MW01687555

Joel Deane was born in Melbourne in 1969. He spent his childhood in the Goulburn Valley and lived in the San Francisco Bay Area for six years. A widely published poet, he has worked as a copyboy, newspaper reporter, editor, TV and Internet producer, press secretary and speechwriter.

A collection of his poetry, ***Subterranean Radio Songs****, was commended for the IP Picks 2004 Award for Best Poetry. Joel has performed at Melbourne's La Mama Poetica, Intersection for the Arts in San Francisco's Mission District and the M.H. de Young Museum in San Francisco's Golden Gate Park.*

Joel lives in Melbourne with his wife and two children and is currently speechwriter for the Premier of Victoria, Steve Bracks.

Another*, which won the IP Picks 2004 Award for Best Fiction, is his first novel.*

The ***Emerging Authors Series*** ***showcases the best Australian emerging literary talent and is available in digital and print form.***

Another

Joel Deane

Interactive Press
Brisbane

Interactive Press
an imprint of Interactive Publications
Treetop Studio • 9 Kuhler Court
Carindale, Queensland, Australia 4152
sales@ipoz.biz
www.ipoz.biz/ip/ip.htm

First published by Interactive Press, 2004

Printed in 12 pt Adobe Jenson Pro on 14 pt Futura by Imprint, Queensland, Australia. Made, printed and bound in Australia.

National Library of Australia
Cataloguing-in-Publication data:

Deane, Joel, 1969- .
Another.

ISBN 1 876819 25 1.

1. Interpersonal relations in adolescence - Fiction.
I. Title. (Series : Emerging authors).

A823.4

for Kirsten, Sophie and Noah

Acknowledgements

Jacket design: David Reiter

Cover photo: Joel Deane

Author Photos: Camille Deane

San Francisco's Intersection for the Arts in general, and Charles Wilmoth in particular, for their support during the early development of this novel.

IP for supporting new and emerging writers.

The staff of IP, Dr David Reiter, Morag Kobez-Halvorson, Sara Moss and Sue Nelson, for kicking my manuscript into publishable shape.

Camille Deane, my cover model and editorial consigliere.

Kirsten Deane, my first and best critic.

Contents

Another

Fire

One

Fire. I see fire: a ball of light consuming and creating. *Fire*. The most brilliant constellation, it fills the black night sky with a long sigh of grey-white smoke, burns itself into my mind's eye. *Fire*. Makes me turn in my womb and kick—kick again.

Fire. The house is burning down. *Fire*. The boy is hiding in the corner of the yard in his sandbox watching his house burn down and the black silhouetted figures dance around, call his name. *Fire*. 'Toby!' they call. *Fire*. 'Tow-bee!' they scream and stare into the flames. *Fire*. A vortex of primary colours. *Fire*. The boy hides in the sandbox as his burnt skin bubbles, turns to glass.

Fire. I see fire—the purest image—so that is where I must begin.

Burning images—looming bright, radiating heat—flash back through Toby Purcell's mind as he stands in the shade of the garage with the battered Yamaha lying at his feet on its side on a blue plastic sheet in the middle of the concrete slab floor. It is his big brother's motorcycle. Danny's bike.

Toby trails a greasy hand through the dirty blonde hair that falls across his grey eyes. It's been shut up for weeks, this place, but still smells of Danny. Oil, rubber, nicotine, and petrol permeate the air.

There's an old black leather motorcycle jacket on a peg beside a pair of grotty overalls. Toby tries it on for size. Well worn, creased around the armpits and elbows, it fits around him like armour, squeaks when he runs his hand through his hair again. Toby crouches, fingers the Yamaha's metal scars and twisted limbs, wonders whether he can bend it back into shape.

'Not today,' Toby tells himself.

It's hot in the garage. The summer sun belts down on the tin roof but the slab floor is morgue cool. Toby zips up Danny's jacket, steps out into the bone-dry afternoon and swings the garage door shut.

The backyard is overgrown. The stripped, rusted carcasses of wrecked cars—Danny's unfinished projects—rest where flowerbeds once bloomed. An ancient aluminium caravan, mounted on bricks instead of wheels, leans hard against the back fence. Toby's sandbox is still there, but holds more weeds than sand these days.

Standing outside, amidst the wreckage, Toby can hear Mum and Michelle bickering. They are at it again. Ever since Danny's accident they've argued over anything—telly, money, Michelle getting a job, Mum getting a life, Michelle's slutty make-up and clothes, Mum's crappy food, Michelle's cleaning duties—anything but Danny. That subject is taboo.

Toby can't make out the words, but, judging by the tones, his mother and his de facto sister-in-law are building to a short, sharp crescendo. Better not be around when the shit hits the fan, he decides.

Besides, Toby has better things to do.

Two

Toby has always hidden his scars. Each inquisitor receives a different, more fantastic explanation.

'What happened to my skin? Well, you see, my spaceship burst into flames when I was reentering earth's atmosphere...My V8 supercar blew a tyre coming down the mountain at Bathurst...I was captured by cannibals and barely escaped...I was a Hollywood stuntman and got dragged behind this car...'

If Danny ever catches anyone asking Toby questions or staring, though, he thumps them. It doesn't matter who they are, Danny'll go after them. He knows how to throw a punch, Danny does, and Toby admires him for it—fears him for it. When he was a kid, at school, Toby slouched like Danny, wore his shirt untucked like Danny, cut his hair short like Danny, but he never stopped being scared of Danny.

It's the fire's fault. The fire changed everything.

Toby remembers lying on his stomach in the Children's Hospital with all the other burns kids, listening to Dr Goldberg tell Mum where he can harvest fresh skin to cover the exposed shoulder blades.

'The thighs and buttocks,' Dr Goldberg says quietly.

'Will it hurt?' Mum asks.

Toby is foxing, pretending to be asleep, peeking through his eyelashes. The two grown-ups are speaking in their normal voices, not the singsong everything's-fine tone they usually put on for his benefit. He strains to hear the surgeon's answer, but Dr Goldberg doesn't speak; instead he either nods ('yes, it will hurt') or shakes ('no, it won't'). It isn't until after the first operation that Toby knows that the doctor nods.

Danny changes after the fire, blames himself for Toby's scars. He quits bullying Toby, turns his guilt onto outsiders—inquisitors—anyone who glances sideways at Toby. They're all fair game. Man, woman or child, it doesn't matter: if they look twice at Toby they cop it. Like Lionel Blackmore. Lionel was a couple of years ahead of Toby and Danny at school, but that didn't matter.

Lionel never saw Danny coming.

This is how it happened.

It's recess and Toby's waiting in line at the kiosk, wearing short sleeves. But Lionel can't stop gawking at the molten skin on his arms.

'Fuck me,' Lionel says. 'What happened to you?'

'Nuthin',' Toby replies.

Everyone in the queue is staring now. A girl next to Lionel squeals—Toby wishes he could douse her in petrol, strike a match.

Lionel perseveres, '*Toby*, tell us.'

Toby shakes his head.

'Yeah, Toby. Come on, please tell us what happened.'

'Well,' Toby says—and is about to launch into his secret-agent-caught-behind-enemy-lines-yarn when Danny barges into the fray. Danny is repeating Year Ten because he punched out the maths teacher, Mr Solvander, for calling him stupid. Dark and lithe, hair shaved back to suede, arms wiry, fists and elbows bony; nobody hassles Danny. Least of all Lionel Blackmore.

Poor Lionel. Danny runs up, leaps forward, spears his elbow into Lionel's face—a human javelin—and he goes down hard, his head snapping back and cracking on the ground, making a sick noise as it bounces on the asphalt.

But Danny doesn't stop there. He kicks Lionel around the head and body until his desert boots are speckled with blood. And he keeps kicking.

It takes three teachers to drag him off Lionel Blackmore.

Three

Beyond the back fence of the Purcell's house, on the edge of the estate, dry razor grass and thistles stretch for kilometres across the paddocks of old Hanlon's farm. The horizon is marred by high-voltage power lines, their pylons marching in Indian-file across the flat paddocks towards the distant, unseen ocean like some invading army. Overhead, a jumbo jet lumbers, banking to make its final run into the new airport runway. Flying low.

Toby walks beside the fence that keeps Hanlon's cattle in, Another out. Toby remembers when Hanlon first electrified the fence. It was back before the fire, when he was a boy riding his hand-me-down BMX through the grass and thistle with Danny.

The two brothers find the new fence and the Do Not Touch sign. Typically, Danny ignores the warning and touches the fence, jumping backwards with a start.

'Does it hurt?' Toby asks.

Danny gives his little brother a shrewd smile: 'Why doncha find out?'

'Nah.'

'Chicken.'

'Na-ah. Got better things to do.'

'Bullshit.'

'All right then.'

Toby throws his bike down in the grass, comes close to touching the wire.

'Stop!' Danny orders.

Toby freezes.

'Not chicken?'

'Nah.'

Danny smiles again: 'Then piss on it.'

Toby's mouth makes funny noises.

'Bo-ck! Bock bock bock!' Danny sticks his hands in his armpits and flaps his chicken wings.

'All right then,' Toby says eventually.

He unzips himself and, after a long wait, pisses on the humming wire.

Toby keeps cutting around the perimeter of the subdivision, past the backsides of the houses. The front subdivisions are full, finished off with lawns, fences, and street lights—but every second or third subdivision in the back blocks is either grass and thistle, with a FOR SALE sign pegged in the middle, or a just-finished brick-veneer shell (no curtains, no carpets) plonked in a raw clay yard.

At the end of the electrified fence is another fallow paddock roped in by rusted barbed wire. Toby places a palm on top of a wooden post, propels himself over the wire, lands up to his armpits in the long grass.

Toby is blind to the future, to the past, but, churning within my womb, I see the paddock as it once was—an ancient ocean of giant eucalyptus trees—and as it will be—a giant car park. Perfectly flat, with newly painted parking bays and creamy-black bitumen that burns the soles of bare feet, the giant car park funnels shoppers into the hallowed halls of a glass-and-concrete behemoth of a shopping mall that shimmers in the heat, dominates the skyline. The giant car park is covered with cars—blanketed—just as a canopy of giant gum trees once enveloped the paddock in a blue-green eucalyptus haze. The bush is gone now, penned into nature strips, backyards, and flowerbeds. The land it once shielded has been baked to a concrete-clay husk, covered with grass, thistle, and electric fences. Toby passes through the grass and thistle paddock, oblivious to the shadows that brim about him in the tall grass—red kangaroos... tiger snakes...giant gum trees...a Koori woman running to hide her baby daughter, her summer dress billowing behind her—brush against him.

Toby does not see the shadows, but I do. I see what has been and gone, leaving a ghostly mark—I see the burning images of what has passed and what is yet to come as I labour to evolve into a form that is fit to be born.

I am not a child. I am a cell dividing. I am a tadpole. I am a catfish. I am a monkey no bigger than Toby's thumb. I am a naked astronaut in zero gravity.

...Above and beyond Houston within my human capsule...out of reach...unable to speak...the sacks of my lungs filled to capacity with amniotic fluid...

I curl myself into a ball. Try to visualize myself, but see only red, hear only the pounding of my toy heart, which beats in time with the concussion of a mammoth heart. My Suzie's heart.

The tom-tom of that greater heart resonates through living flesh.

It comforts me.

Four

On the far side of the paddock sits a twenty-four hour service station and a McDonald's. Toby climbs the fence, slouches across the car park toward the McDonald's Drive-Thru menu board, leans on the fibreglass ORDER HERE box, waits a beat, squints at the cashier's window, then, finally, bends over and says 'hullo' into the microphone.

'Whadda you want?' The fibreglass contraption squawks back.

'Quarterpoundermealdeal.'

'Where's yer car?'

'Jeez.'

'Order inside.'

'Come on Suzie.'

'Piss off Toby. You'll get me in trouble.'

Toby gesticulates at the cashier's window: 'Who with?'

'Brendan.'

'Fuck Brendan.'

'Fuck *off*.'

Toby walks up the Drive-Thru ramp, sticks his head through the cashier's window.

'You're s'posed to ask me if I wanna sundae,' he says.

The cashier sneaks a look behind her before she grants Toby a kiss on the lips. A short, pert kiss.

'S'pose you're broke?' she asks.

'S'pose...come on Suzie.'

Suzie's eyes, which are hazel and outlined with black mascara, dart over Toby's face, which is young and dirty and bitter to kiss.

She arches an eyebrow: 'Where'd you get the jacket?'

He shrugs: 'M'brother.'

She nods. Walks wordlessly from the register back into the white-tiled recesses of the kitchen, returns with the shadow of a smile. Suzie is strikingly pale, her milk-white skin made starker by her heavy mascara and chocolate lipstick.

'Orright,' she says. 'But this is the last time.'

'Ta, Suzie.'

Toby kisses her again, but Suzie pretends she's preoccupied with the till. He slouches to the next window. Another cashier sporting heavy mascara gives him a conspiratorial nod as she stuffs a Quarter Pounder into a brown paper bag.

'Hi Jenny,' Toby says.

Jenny allows herself a nervous smile. Brendan, the manager, is standing behind her shoulder at the front counter; his stomach resting on the till as he serves three large Big Mac meal deals. He's none the wiser.

'Enjoy your meal, and have a nice day,' Jenny singsongs with a wink.

Five

Toby sits in one of the Drive Thru's waiting bays. Devouring his Quarter Pounder, fries, and Coke. Wiping his hands on his jeans. Waiting for Suzie.

Toby and Suzie have been going out for a few months. They started talking one night outside the servo, walked a kilometre down the two-lane highway, kicked stones in front of themselves, compared their favourite movies (she liked *Matrix*, he liked *Black Hawk Down*), went halvies on a cask of wine at the bottle shop, found a dark patch of grass, squirted long slashes of wine into each other's open mouths, kissed, fucked, fell into a dizzy sleep as the Earth revolved beneath them. Next day Suzie showed Toby where she'd carved his name into her inner thigh.

Suzie is always asking Toby about his scars.

'How'd you get them? Did they hurt? Did you like it? Didja do 'em y'self? Do you touch them much? Do you like touching them? Can I touch them? Are they sensitive? Would you give someone else scars?'

And Toby always shrugs, says 'no'—which only makes Suzie more curious.

Suzie comes out of the employees' exit, cigarette in hand. She strikes her Bic...lights up...draws hard...glances at Toby...ambles over.

'Hi,' he says.

'Hi y'self.'

He offers a half-eaten Quarter Pounder. 'Want some?'

Suzie grimaces: 'Nup. I hate McDonald's.'

'Wanna go for a walk?'

'Where?'

'Dunno.'

Suzie shrugs. They head for the paddock, sit cross-legged at the edge of the car park, backs to the barbed-wire fence.

'How's work?'

'Shit. Brendan's a prick. *Do this. Do that. Don't forget to ask 'em whether or not they want a drink with their burger or a sundae with their drink. Smile more. Stand straight. Say, Have a nice day.* Fuck me dead, it's worse than school.'

'Cept you get paid.'

'Yeah, Brendan's such a fat yuppie arsehole, but. He goes around sucking up to the customers, telling Mr Longo how much he wants to own his own Maccas franchise, then yells at us when there's no-one around—'

'Prick.'

'—he even made Jenny cry the other day. She gets yelled at by some slag cos she'd served her cold fries. The slag goes, *I'm gunna sue! It nearly made me sick! Wait'll Ronald fucken McDonald hears about this*—'

'Bitch.'

'—stupid slag bitch. Real bright. An' Brendan comes out from the kitchen and asks what the problem is an' tells the stupid slag bitch he's gunna sack Jenny an' Jenny starts crying an' the stupid slag bitch goes, *Oh no, I think she's learnt her lesson.* So she ups an' walks out. Jenny's bawling her eyes out and I'm yellin' at Brendan, callin' him a prick—'

'He's a mongrel.'

'—an' he just stares at me, real nasty, the shit, an' goes, *You better watch it.* Jenny says she wants to baptize him in the deep fry...'

Suzie allows herself a harsh laugh, then settles, concentrates on her cigarette. Toby watches. She's a fast, nervous smoker.

'What?' Suzie asks.

'Huh?'

She butts her cigarette out on the concrete curb: 'You're lookin'. What is it?'

'Nuthin'.'

'Orright, then,' Suzie says. 'I don't give a shit.'

She lets Toby stare at her. She lights up another cigarette—goes glassy eyed as she fills her chest cavity with blue smoke. Before she finishes her ciggie, though, Toby's talking again.

He blurts it out: 'I'm gunna fix Danny's bike.'

'What?'

'His bike. I'm gunna fix it all up an' take you for a ride. We might even go to the city. Whadda y'think?'

'Didn't know you were a mechanic.'

'I'm not. But I helped Danny sometimes, you know, watched him work. It's easy enough.'

'Uh-huh,' Suzie says, mind wafting.

'D'you want me to come an' get you tonight?' Toby asks.

Suzie doesn't answer.

'Suzie?'

'I heard. Come round to my joint later.'

Suzie kisses Toby on the mouth. She tastes like tobacco and french fries. Involuntarily, he gets an erection; nurses it as his girlfriend walks back to finish her shift.

Dusk approaches as Toby walks home beside the electric fence. He sees women cooking dinner; teenagers and fathers watching television; bare-chested young men soaking up the last of the sunshine as they hose down Commodores, Falcons, WRXes, and Monaros.

The cicadas start up in the long grass, singing louder as sunset approaches. It's January, the height of summer, and the drought has people gossiping about water restrictions and bushfires. Toby glides along the fence, taking everything in.

A barbecue is cooking nearby; the scent of burning flesh makes his mouth water.

Six

Pissing against the electric fence is like coming—white light—a bone-shaking sensation, but with more pain than pleasure.

Toby ends up lying on his mother's double bed, looking straight up as she inspects the damage with dry, efficient hands. Danny is out in the kitchen. Staring at the ceiling, Toby can hear his brother chattering at Gran.

'There was smoke coming off his balls! You shoulda seen it!' Danny crows.

The pinch grip on Toby's penis tightens as Mum yells down the hall: 'Danny! Watch y'mouth!'

A feeble 'Sorry' drifts back.

'Stay there.'

Mum marches into the bathroom. Rummages about. Returns with her jar of magic green Kiwi cream, which she rubs into his aching testicles, ignoring all protestations.

Seven

As a boy—before the fire—Toby believed in ghosts. He would lie in bed, straining to hear them. Run to the window whenever he thought he heard a noise. Turn on the light, check under the bed, if he thought there was something in the room. He believed, Toby did. And he reckoned Mum believed too. She was always on the lookout, flicking on the outside light, going out with her best carving knife in her fist, drifting in and out of Danny and Toby's room when she thought they were asleep, telling them to never talk to strangers.

Toby was sure he saw a ghost once at the supermarket. He was sitting in the seat of the shopping cart, facing Mum. Danny was dragging his feet alongside, whining for an ice cream. And Mum was pushing the cart as she pulled cut-price items from the shelves and told Danny to stop grizzling. Mum was steering up the aisle, towards the frozen food section, when she froze.

That's when Toby looked up.

He saw Mum's face, usually so hard to read, shuttered, flung wide open. She was staring straight ahead—mouth open, bug-eyed—just like Toby reckoned you'd do if you saw a ghost. Then she yanked Toby up out of the shopping cart; held him to her hip with one arm, dragged Danny behind her with the other, as she ran round in circles. Toby could feel her ragged breathing as they scuttled out a service exit, weaved through the storage area until it emptied into the car park. All the while, Mum didn't speak. She fluttered; chest rattling with ragged, shallow breathing as she roared out of the car park and barrelled down the highway.

Eight

Toby climbs the back fence, heads for the backdoor. Mum is waiting in the kitchen, arms folded. She is a small woman, Mum. Short and dark, with olive skin, brown eyes, and a nose that wasn't properly reset the last time it was broken. She looks nothing like her youngest son, who is the picture of his father. It's a resemblance Mum tries to not hold against Toby, although she's always felt more connected to Danny.

'Where y'been?' she asks before the screen door has a chance to crack shut.

'Out.'

'Uh-huh.'

She takes a long look at Danny's leather jacket, says, 'Dinner's ready.'

Toby heads into the lounge. Michelle and Gran are on the couch, watching a rerun of *Roseanne*.

'Hi Gran,' Toby says and flops into an armchair with foam bulging from its ruined arms.

Gran ignores her grandson, stares benignly at the telly's furry picture—a pale blue crocheted beanie pulled tight over her eggshell of a scone.

Nothing matches in this house: everything is either broken, worn out, or borrowed. The windows are flung open, but the feeble breeze barely dints the years of compounded smoke, ash, and dust.

Michelle is smoking, chin sunk into her jowls, flicking the ash into a dirty coffee mug, watching the telly through blue mascara squint-holes. Roseanne lets rip with a one-liner about loose-meat sandwiches and the show chops into an ad-break, but Gran keeps staring at the screen. Still squinting, Michelle turns away, zeroes in on Toby.

'That's Danny's jacket.'

'Yep.'

'So why're you wearing it?'

'Cos I like it.'

Her voice trails off: 'Danny liked it too.'

'*Likes*,' Mum corrects from the kitchen, making Michelle roll her eyes.

Toby watches an ad where suntanned skydivers jump from a plane brandishing surfboards, then air-surf down to a soft drink machine. Michelle squints hard at Toby through a haze of smoke as the ad washes impassively over him.

'You need a haircut,' she says when the ad concludes. 'Something to even out the length, you know, tidy it up a bit. Get it layered. You could look half-decent then.' Michelle nods her head as though agreeing with herself: 'An' if you started washing your hair sometimes—maybe even ran some colour through it, lighten it, you know—then you'd look half orright.'

'No thanks,' he says with a bored yawn—eyes riveted to the telly.

Michelle gives Toby a carnivorous smile: 'What? Scared of losing your scum appeal? You don't have a girlfriend, d'you?'

Toby puts all his focus on the telly.

Mum comes in from the kitchen: 'Leave Toby be.'

'What for? I'm tryin' to help.'

'Help yourself first. Get a fucken job.'

Michelle bares her teeth: 'Y'know, I might just do that. I could've been a hairdresser, y'know. That's what I wanted t'be.'

'No one's stoppin' you,' Mum says and shuffles back into the kitchen.

Nine

Tea time. Gran, Mum, Michelle, and Toby eat in front of the telly, mismatched plates on their laps. Gran, Michelle, and Mum are squeezed onto the couch, Toby cross-legged on the floor. Gran picks feebly at her food. Mum, hungry, but too tired to eat heartily, talks over the telly, firing questions at Toby and Michelle about their activities during the day. Both give monosyllabic responses. Michelle eats out of spite, wishing she had more money, wishing Gran didn't stink of piss, wishing they could have afforded a takeaway pizza. Toby is voracious—shovelling down two serves of Mum's special fried rice, topped off with lashings of soy sauce and lime cordial.

After *Roseanne* Toby changes the channel with a pair of pliers—the dial has snapped off, leaving just a metal stub to manipulate—to watch *Big Brother*. Mum falls asleep mid-sentence and Michelle starts up in her stead, giving a running commentary on the foibles of the *Big Brother* contestants. Gran, perched at one end of the couch with her fried rice still on her lap, feeds herself one grain at a time. Toby lies on his back, soles of his feet planted either side of the TV screen, and lets the telly's furry colours—reds, blues, browns, oranges, yellows, greens—wash over him.

It's dark by the time Toby goes out to his caravan, but his feet know their way through the debris. Inside the van, he turns on the light, flops on the bunk with his head in his hands, sees the colour yellow—a blinding yellow canvas. *Danny*.

He tries to think of Suzie, but sees Danny in his leathers and helmet, caught in mid-air, a doll thrown against a blinding yellow canvas of a sky. Utterly rudderless, out of control. Then Toby sees nothing—hears the impact of leather and blood and tissue and bone striking steel.

Ten

Morning. Mum knocks once on the caravan exterior before barging in and tripping over a pile of clothes on the floor.

'Shit!' She picks herself up: 'Y'been in Danny's garage?'

Toby grunts from bed.

'Everything orright?'

'Bit dusty, but, yeah, orright.'

'An' y'like Danny's jacket.'

'Yeah. It, y'know, it smells like him.'

Mum starts sorting through the washing as he talks, separating dark T-shirts from white.

'I'm gunna fix the bike,' Toby declares.

Mum nods: 'Good, Danny likes that bike.'

'Yeah.'

'He's always looked after it...'

Mum stops talking, casts her eyes around the van: '...You done something different in here? Ah—the stereo.'

'What?'

Mum points at the black mini-stereo sitting on the bench—equipped with a CD player and double tape deck.

'You're not stealing again are you Toby?'

'Nah. I bought it.'

'Where?'

Toby starts to wind himself up: 'Second-hand, orright? Wanna see my receipt?'

'No. No, I don't.'

'I bought it. That stereo cost me, ah, a hundred-and-fifty bucks, easy.'

'And where didja find—' Mum cuts herself off, backs off. 'Fine,' she says with resignation, 'Fine.'

'I bought it,' Toby says, trying to sound emphatic.

'Fine.'

Mum moves clumsily across the cluttered floor, touches Toby's face. He blinks in such a way it resembles a flinch. Mum retreats to the doorway, gathering an armful of dark washing from the floor as she goes, asks Toby whether he's going out.

'Yep.'

'Oh...Michelle's goin' out too.'

'Who with?'

'Some girlfriend. Anyway, Gran'll be orright while I'm at work.'

'Orright, then.'

'Fine, then. Fine. I'll leave you be.'

'Fine.'

'You enjoy yourself then, but...'

'—but be careful. Yep, okay.'

'Fine, then.'

'Fine.'

Toby listens to Mum's thongs click their way back to the house. A jet rumbles overhead, making the table vibrate. Toby waits until he hears the old Kingswood reverse down the drive.

Eleven

Toby walks briskly through the estate's sporadically lit streets until he reaches Suzie's house; stands in the darkness, breathing lightly. Suzie Collier's house is in the front half of the estate. Her house is a white-brick veneer affair, with window-bays on the upper floor jutting out in every direction like melanomas. Two white concrete lions stand guard atop the concrete gateposts; waiting between the lions, cross-legged in the driveway, sits Suzie.

She stands as Toby approaches.

'How was work? Any trouble?' Toby asks.

Suzie shakes her head. Her McDonald's uniform has been shed, replaced by boots, faded black jeans and a black T-shirt. The silhouette of someone, probably Suzie's stepmother, Mrs Collier, loiters at one of the upper floor's windows.

'So, where're we goin'?'

Suzie stretches, says with a yawn: 'The servo.'

Suzie and Toby slouch off, hands stuffed into the pockets of their jeans, not touching. They are barely around the corner before Suzie's mobile phone bleats: *Beepbeep! Beepbeep!*

'Fuck,' Suzie hisses and pulls out the contraption.

DON'T B L8 HOME & DON'T SMOKE. LUV MUM, the SMS reads.

'Yeah right,' Suzie replies.

Beepbeep! Beepbeep! **& SAY HI 2 TOBY**.

Suzie relays her stepmother's greeting to Toby.

'Say hi right back,' Toby mumbles.

'As if.'

Suzie and Toby weave through the estate's streets toward the servo, cutting across a vacant subdivision, walking beside a long line of back fences marred by fresh graffiti spray-painted in red: ONE NATION...ONE RACE...KILL ILLEGAL GOOKS...WIN THE RACE WAR 4 OUR SHORE...

The service station is a neon island surrounded by the darkness of Another.

A new Honda, shiny and red, is parked behind McDonald's.

'Nice car,' Toby notes.

Suzie nods: 'Brendan's car.'

'Where's Brendan?'

'Closing up, prob'ly.'

Toby smiles slyly: 'I oughta take it for a fang.'

'Go on, then. Go on,' Suzie coaxes.

Toby scouts around the deserted car park. Only the servo is nearby, but that's on the other side of the building and the car is parked in the outermargins of the darkness.

'Where's Brendan?'

'Inside, I toldja.'

'...Oh.'

'Go on.'

'...Nah.'

'*Toby*.'

'What?'

'Go on. We could be on the freeway by now.'

'You do it then.'

'Aw—forget it. Fucken forget it.'

Bored again, Suzie trudges across to the servo.

Groups of teenagers are gathered around, talking in twos and threes, smoking cigarettes, swigging from communal bottles of Coke. Suzie hurries ahead of Toby, hugs Jenny.

'Hi Toby,' Jenny calls.

He waves back.

'Jeez I'm bored,' Suzie sighs, then starts telling Jenny what Toby didn't have the 'nads to do.

Toby drifts away from the two girls, muddling through his pockets for money. He has fifty cents, not enough for a Coke. He looks around. These are Suzie's friends. Kids. He's at least a year older than most of them. Toby doesn't want to ask these kids for a swig of their Coke. He wants his own jumbo-sized bottle of Coke. He wants them to ask him for a drink. He glances at Suzie—who's still telling Jenny how much of a bastard Brendan is, how much of a dick-less wonder Toby is—walks into the servo's Shopping Mart.

The automatic doors hum open, hum shut.

The cashier, a bald man with glasses so thick they magnify his eyeballs to the size of golf balls, hunches over the counter, watches Toby graze slowly between the aisles, through the confectionery, toiletries, video rental, tinned food, car-care, drinks, and ice cream sections; pause at the magazine stand. He flicks through dog-eared copies of *Soldier of Fortune* and *Wheels,* toys with a *Penthouse.*

'You right?' the cashier calls.

Toby shoves the *Penthouse* back into the stand: 'Yep.'

'Gunna buy anything? This isn't a library, y'know.'

'D'you have *Black Hawk Down?*'

'What magazine's that?'

'It's a movie.'

'Ah,' says the cashier with a drawn out sigh as his billiard-ball eyes refuse to blink, 'Are you a member?'

'Yeah, course,' Toby lies. He blinks hard at the cashier, ambles outside.

Outside, Toby loiters; eventually falling into a discussion with a kid called Sal. Sal, who has two earrings in his right eyebrow; Sal, who is pale and heavily freckled, with an edgy, rodent body; Sal, who buckles up his fists, white knuckled, and says, 'All Asians must die.'

Sal jigs his leg, darts his eyes around, talks fast: 'My big brother—right?—he got beat up by these fucken ninjas in the city. Cunts! They're fucken everywhere, mate. We gotta stop 'em before there's too many of 'em...It's like that movie, y'know, *Romper Stomper,* we gotta beat the shovelheads before they beat us. Fight back—right?—stop th'fucken Asian invasion.'

Sal rabbits on at Toby for an hour, running through his them-or-us thesis until he stops abruptly and takes off with a nervous jig of a walk into the darkness. Left to his own devices, Toby paces the perimeter of the servo, touches every pump, runs his fingertips over every shiny surface—watches Suzie, cross-legged on the concrete, smoke and talk incessantly to Jenny.

He could watch her all night.

Twelve

The first time Toby fucked Suzie he didn't know what to think.

Toby had never fucked anyone before, never thought anyone would want to touch, let alone kiss, his molten skin. Yet there he was, kissing Suzie. And there was Suzie, kissing him, feeling his scars.

Toby stuck his hand up Suzie's T-shirt, fumbled around in an alcoholic daze. He slipped down the front of her pants, poked a finger in her slot.

Suzie unbuttoned his jeans.

She swung one leg over and started bucking about on top.

And Toby lay there—not quite sure what was supposed to happen next.

Thirteen

Suzie and Toby walk in silence through the long grass and thistles, leave a trail of shadows in their wake.

'Tell me something,' Suzie finally says.

'What?'

'Tell me about your arms and back.'

'This again.'

'Toby. I wanna know cos they're part of you. An' I like you.'

'So?'

'So. I like you; I like your scars...'

'Pig's arse.'

'Tell me.'

She tugs at Danny's jacket, makes Toby stop walking. Her hand slips under his T-shirt. Her fingers trace the scar tissue that marks where the surgeons sutured skin grafts over his raw shoulder blades. Toby pulls away.

'Don't you like it?' Suzie sounds offended.

'Dunno.'

'Dunno what? Don't you like me touching you?'

'But you just wanna touch my scars. Why don't you touch my face?'

Suzie tries to touch Toby's face, but he grabs her hard by the wrists, holds her at a safe distance. Toby is taller and stronger than Suzie—her eyes flare, she tries to shake herself free.

'Lemme go,' she demands.

He holds fast.

'Lemme go!'

He tightens his grip.

'LET ME GO!'

Suzie's scream booms across the paddock, shoots into the stars. Toby lets go and Suzie punches him hard, throwing a right that connects sweetly with his jaw.

Toby falls back into the grass, but leaps back up—furious, swearing.

'FUCKEN BITCH! What's wrong with you?!'

'WITH ME?! WITH ME?!' And Suzie is swinging punches again, forcing Toby to back away, fend off her blows which are half-hearted now. Finally, Suzie stops swinging. Stands there, breathing hard.

'Fuck you!' Suzie huffs and puffs. 'FUCK YOU!'

'Me! What did I do? WHAT DID I DO?!'

Suzie pants for air. Fists clenched. Glaring.

'What's the matter with you?' he asks, bewildered.

She hisses: 'You shouldn't grab someone like that. You shouldn't ever grab someone like that.'

Toby takes a step toward Suzie: 'Grab what?'

Tears swell in Suzie's eyes.

'Oh, fuck! Not now!' she yells, backs away.

Suzie tries to, but she cannot stop the tears. She stands there, glaring at Toby—defiant—as she dissolves.

Toby has seen Suzie smoke a cigar, seen her steal a fully-laden shopping trolley from Safeway, seen her call a bus driver a 'fuckendumbassmotherfucker', seen her skull a can of bourbon and Coke, seen her piss in a car park between two Taragos, seen her suck his dick by torchlight, seen her throw-up in a movie theatre without making a sound, seen her mutilate herself with a razor—but he has never seen her cry.

Transfixed, Toby watches her cry for a long time. Waits for her to run dry.

Finally he whispers: 'I don't understand.'

Fourteen

If Toby's complete history is burnt into his skin, Suzie's redacted version is carved out of hers. Pieces are missing. Her images and memories are the smallest pieces of an incomplete puzzle—cutaways of a much larger picture.

Her mother. Vanishing like some wicked witch. Kissing her daughter goodnight before she shoots through in her husband's company car; he, in turn, carting armfuls of his runaway wife's belongings—clothes, photographs, jewelry, electric toothbrush—out to the incinerator. Dousing the lot in kerosene. By the time the flames die out all that remains are a matching pair of pumps that fall from the fire, smoulder side by side on the ground. Is that where Mum stood when she exploded? Suzie thinks.

Every birthday since the disappearance, from six upwards, a card appears in the mail with a twenty dollar bill folded inside and a biro inscription ('Mummy loves you from afar,' 'I am always near to you in my heart,' 'Look for my footsteps beside you in the sand,' 'Never trust a man who says, *Trust me*'), but it is Monopoly money to Suzie—New Zealand currency posted from Wellington with no return address. She stockpiles the cards, throws the money away.

Her father. By day an attack dog. By night a mongrel dog on heat. The steel wool of his chin brushing against the soft skin of her arm, her thigh, her breast—all the places she would later need to cut clean—together with the stink of his adult body. Now that she's outgrown him, Suzie can no longer look her father in the eye, because if she sees him staring at a part of her she feels obliged—compelled—to cut that part clean.

Mrs Collier. A female storm-trooper beneath a helmet of permed hair. The bitch who let Suzie's dog of a father roam the house as he pleased.

A steel stationary compass. Cradled in a child's bloodstained hand it carves crisscross shapes into Suzie's inner thigh.

'Jeez. Forget it.'

Suzie sniffs, rubs her eyes: 'Fuck. I've got mascara everywhere.'

'You look like Marilyn Manson.'

'Who?' Suzie frowns, climbs to her feet.

They start for home again, walking a little further apart than before.

'So, you like my scars,' Toby ventures.

Suzie snorts.

'Do you?'

'I said so, didn't I?'

'Yeah.'

'Yeah. I want one.'

'One what?'

'A scar. Like a tribal mark, y'know?'

'What?'

'A scar.'

'You serious?'

'Course. People get nose jobs an' boob jobs. I wanna scar job.'

Toby scratches his head. Suzie picks up her pace, walking ahead, tracing the wooden fence palings with her fingertips.

'Do you know what I wanna do?' Suzie asks.

'What?' Toby sounds hopeful.

'No. Not that—we'd catch foot rot if we fucked in the paddocks.'

'Oh.'

'America. I wanna go to Hollywood and hang out with Keanu.'

'Uh-huh.'

'An' I wanna go to...ah...New York. I wanna be an actress or something like that. Y'know, be famous, go to parties an' get my picture taken, get put on telly. My real mum's living in LA. She's nearly got an actress job on one of those soap operas. When she gets on telly she's going to buy me a ticket to America and we're going to live in Hollywood an' I'll go to Disneyland on the weekends.' Suzie pauses. 'D'you think I should get my nipples pierced?'

Toby is no longer listening. He catches a shadow movement in the corner of his eye...a naked Koori boy swimming in thin air...and stops dead.

Suzie keeps walking and talking: '...or should I get a tattoo on my shoulder blade?'

He spins around, scans the darkness.

She keeps thinking aloud until she realizes she's alone: 'Toby? What're y'doin'?'

Toby watches the shadow of a slender boy frog kick past, gliding just above the grass, swimming with the breeze.

'Toby?'

'What?'

'I'm bored shitless. We should do something.'

'What?'

'Anything.'

Suzie's feeling reckless; her eyes are wild again.

'We could go back to my caravan,' Toby suggests.

'Typical.'

'No—I've got a new CD player...haven't got any CDs, but.'

'Where'd you get a CD player?'

'I found it.'

'Bullshit.'

'No bullshit.'

'Where'd y'find it?'

'In a house.'

'Whose house?'

Toby shrugs: 'A house.'

'What were y'doin' in a house?'

'Lookin'.'

'Didja take anything for me?'

'Nup. I didn't see anything good enough.'

Fifteen

The first time Suzie fucked Toby she was drunk.

She was drunk and riding on top of him like some rodeo rider, squeezing Toby tight between her thighs to stop herself from being thrown clear by the centrifugal force of the Earth, which spun beneath her. She held the reins of his dirty hair and bent low, kissing his closed eyes with her open lips.

Suzie was drunk, but she was thinking.

She was thinking as she fucked.

As she fucked she was thinking she could like this Toby boy more than a lot.

Sixteen

Night. Gliding through the estate, catching glimpses of other lives over fences, through windows and open doors...a husband and wife slump on a couch, spellbound by the blue light of their TV...a child makes a tent out of her sheet, reads *Dolly* magazine by torchlight...a teenager undresses in front of his bedroom mirror, watches himself flex his muscles...

At times like these Toby still believes in ghosts. Childhood nights spent in his room—straining to see or hear what was lurking in the backyard, tapping on his window, hiding beneath his bed—come rushing back.

But it is different now: now Toby is one of the shadows. Effortless, invisible, Toby moves through the streets, swallowed by the darkness until he approaches his house and sees the car.

It's a new car. A Honda Civic with two people inside parked a few doors shy of the Purcell's house.

Toby crosses the road, sits in the gutter just beyond the reach of the street light. He can see Michelle. She is in the car. She is kissing someone other than Danny. He sits. He waits. Finally, Michelle opens the passenger door.

And the interior light flicks on.

Toby knows the driver.

Seventeen

It is hot tonight. Too hot for Gran.

She feels the heat. It sends her shuffling around the house; slipping past Toby, asleep on the couch—the contents of his coffee mug staining the worn carpet.

Gran can't sleep so she turns on the telly.

When she first felt her body letting go, Gran was scared. She thought, My life is over. I am abandoned.

Everything shades into grey. Gran wears woollen cardigans, even in humidity, thinks about turning back and clinging to life, clawing for every day, fighting everyone and everything, especially the doctors at the clinic who only ever want the imprint of her Medicare card, her signature on the bulk-billing form.

But after a while Gran's eyes grow accustomed to the dark. She begins to see the shadows around her, in the house, in the street—elbow-to-elbow in the corridors and wards of the hospital—echoing the movements once made by their concrete selves. And, slowly, the shadows milling about her begin to blend with her own shadow.

Gran is leaving. Her body is letting go of her and she is letting go of her body. She is forsaking concrete life. Her body is old. So much older than its sixty-two years. Her lungs are gone. Emphysema.

Sometimes she forgets, Gran does. Forgets Danny, Toby, Michelle, Jacki, herself...It's the lack of oxygen, she tells herself. Not enough fresh air getting to the brain.

As her body lets go, Gran is letting go, quitting petty regrets. Pa's weaknesses—the grog, the gambling, the open-handed slaps, the jealousy—forgiven or forgotten. Her feuds with Jacki—over the baby, over Gary—beyond redemption. Her hopes—winning Tattslotto, travelling to London, flying on a plane—redundant. None of it matters. Everything is falling away.

Gran relives episodes from her life: black-and-white times, crackling newsreels, an LP record with scratches and grooves where the needle catches....

Like working in the biscuit factory with Rose and Vera...

Smelling the oven is enough to trigger memories of lunch in the loading bay. Sharing fags, chatting up the boys, Pete or Stan or Dougie. Giggling at the way old Harry Higginbottom paraded about the factory floor in his foreman's regalia, checking himself in every reflective surface, even when he was talking to underlings, to ensure his long flap of hair was adequately slicked over his shiny scalp.

The record needle skates round and round Gran's memory.

A black-and-white movie is showing on the telly. It's about three girls having a holiday at the beach, drinking pints of beer, chatting to boys on the foreshore, going to the dances at the yacht club—but it isn't make believe. It's real. She is watching herself on one of her famous long weekends away with Vera and Rose. But, whereas Vera and Rose remain young—the camera lingering on their firm bodies as they parade in their swimming costumes—Gran is painfully old and shrivelled, wearing a nightie and crocheted beanie.

There is another scene at a local dance. That's where Gran meets a young man with slicked-back hair, olive skin and milk chocolate eyes. He says his name is Jack and takes an instant shine to Gran. Jack and Gran talk and laugh and dance and drink and end up on the beach—alone—and it's late and Jack tells Gran he loves her and Gran's head feels like fairy-floss when they kiss and the soundtrack swells and Gran tells Jack she has a boyfriend (young Dougie) and Jack says 'no worries' and unbuttons her in places she has never been unbuttoned before and tells her things she has never heard before, will never hear again.

Eighteen

'Shit,' Mum mutters as she steers the Kingswood up the drive.

She's arrived home early from work, fighting off the first starbursts of a migraine, only to find Gran standing in the glare of her headlights, babbling to herself.

At least she's not on the freeway this time, Mum thinks.

A few months ago Gran walked out the front door in her slippers and nightie and found her way down to the freeway. That's where Gran became confused—mistaking the road for a dance floor, the headlights for spotlights, the wailing horns for a brass band—and waltzed across the lanes of speeding cars. Gran twirling and twirling on the dance floor with Jack's hand hard against the small of her back. She laughed at the blaring horns, thought the cars colliding was the drummer, clung graciously to the arm of the constable who escorted her from the scene of the accident, kept calling him 'my Jack'.

Mum rips on the handbrake, kills the motor, keeps the headlights blazing.

'What're y'doin' you silly old tart?' she calls.

Mum gets out from behind the wheel, walks over and shakes Gran by the shoulder, as though trying to roughly remind her of a missed appointment.

'Jacki?'

'Yeah,' Mum replies, annoyed. 'What're you doin' out here?'

'What's the car doin' in the ballroom?'

'Shit-a-brick. I'm gunna have to start locking you inside again.'

Mum guides Gran back inside. Into her room. Snibs the door shut.

Toby's still asleep on the couch. Mum wakes him and tells him to go to bed. She eases Michelle's door open—she is spread-eagled on her back, snoring.

'Kids,' Mum huffs under her breath.

She heads for the bathroom, searching for a painkiller.

Nineteen

Suzie's lying in the centre of her parents' perfect lawn, staring at the stars. She had been in her room, staring at her ceiling, but decided it would be better to stare at the stars, more dramatic. So now she's out here, flat against the grass, contemplating suicide.

Suzie finds suicide attractive—a seductive alternative. She thinks: Living this life is like being a crash test dummy caught in slow-mo—knowing, as each frame passes, that the inevitable collision is another frame closer.

Next morning she is sitting in her psychiatrist's office. No couch to lie on, no stars painted on the ceiling; just Suzie and her shrink sitting either side of a shin-high coffee table in oversized armchairs. A box of tissues sit, perfectly placed, in the centre of the table.

Dr Wren keeps asking Suzie about whether her mutilations are suicide attempts. She asks, then sits, tapping her pen, lips arranged into a faint smile. She speaks in a tone that intends to soothe, that instead provokes. Suzie loathes Dr Wren's gushing monotone, imagines nailing a compass through that pink tongue. The image makes her smile.

'What's so amusing?'

Suzie's looks up: 'Nothing...My boyfriend. He cracks me up.'

'That's nice, now onto more weighty matters. What conclusions have you come to about your violent episodes?'

'Dr Wren...'

'No, Suzie, just call me Rhonda. Just Rhonda.'

'Well, *Rhonda*,' Suzie says with great deliberation, 'Toby is a very weighty matter to me. Orright?'

'Why?'

'Why? He just is, *Rhonda*.'

'Why are you avoiding our original topic?'

'I'm not avoiding nothin'. I'm just standing up for Toby.'

'What do you mean by that?'
'What?'
'Standing up.'
'Dunno. Looking out for, I suppose.'
'Does he stand up for you?'
'Nope.'
'Why?'
'Cos he doesn't have to. I look after myself.'

Twenty

After they fucked for the first time, Suzie and Toby lay beneath the stars, drifting away from each other, toward sleep. He asked her what she'd do if she had one wish. 'Whaddabout three wishes?' she yawned.

'One wish.'

'Why only one?'

'Don't be greedy.'

'Orright, then...Disneyland.'

'Disneyland?'

'Yep. I wanna go to Disneyland and go on all the rides. That's my wish.'

Toby watched the sky for a while, then asked Suzie whether or not she wanted to hear his one wish, but she didn't reply.

She was already asleep.

Suzie was ten-years-old. She was sitting in class. The compass felt substantial in her hand. She was trying to get inside herself, turn herself inside out, but Annette Norman, teacher's pet, noticed. Miss Munro had made Suzie and Annette share a desk in the hope that Annette's bubbly personality might be contagious. It wasn't. The two girls ignored each other until that day, when Annette saw the compass crisscross Suzie's thighs, saw the crisscrosses draw beads, then ribbons, of blood, which intersected; saw Suzie smear blood on her fingertips, then lick the pads of her fingers clean—taste herself.

Annette Norman's hand shot up.

Miss Munro pointed with her chalk: 'Yes, Annette?'

And that's when Annette Norman dobbed, started blubbering about how Suzie was mutilating herself. The betrayal did not last. Mid-sentence, Suzie stabbed Annette Norman in her pretty little blonde-bobbed face with the compass—leaving the weapon quivering in her left cheek as though it were a bolt fired from a crossbow. All the girls, and most of the boys, screamed. Annette Norman fainted. Miss Munro puked on the polished floorboards: her vomit the consistency of watery mustard.

They suspended Suzie for two weeks. When she returned to school, she found herself parked in a desk by herself, right under Miss Munro's nose. No one spoke to her. Come recess and lunchtime Suzie took her compass and walked to the furthest boundary of the playground. Sitting alone in the dirt with her compass, she carved stars and hearts and dirty words.

Suzie cries herself dry.

'You orright?' Toby asks.

'What?'

'...I never seen you cry before.'

Suzie rubs her eyes with the heel of her hand.

'You shouldn't go grabbing people,' she says.

Toby briefly puts his hands on his hips, then folds his arms until he appears to be hugging himself: 'Well, you shouldn't go mental.'

'Why not? Who says?'

Shadows

One

'Danny!' Toby gasps and jolts awake.

It is late morning; the low sun is flat against the back of the aluminium caravan, cooking the interior. A squadron of flies buzz in the stale air.

Danny. The image of him in his leathers—falling through space—stays in Toby's dreams. Toby feels Danny falling for hours through his dreams and then, just as impact is an instant away, jolts awake. Suspended within my membrane, within Suzie, the expectation of impact makes me jump, too.

Toby pulls on a pair of filthy jeans, stumbles out of the van in bare feet, takes a long slash into the sandbox.

He scratches the back of his neck, fingers a ridge of tissue that marks where the fire first bit. The molten skin on his upper back, down each arm to the elbow, maps the extent of the damage, recalls the time spent in specialists' surgeries, hospital beds, operating theatres, physiotherapists' suites, and psychologists' chairs. The scars on his thighs and backside tell of the repair job, the beating of a boy's body back into shape. He remembers how, after each operation, Mum would tell him that beauty was more than skin deep, that he was the most beautiful boy in Another.

A jet scuds overhead, heading for the airport.

Toby leans back, gawks. What is it? A jumbo? Where's it coming from? How many people does it carry in its belly? How does it stay up there—all those tons of steel?

Danny'd know. He'd know it all. If he were here, Danny would stick a cigarette in his mouth, light it at his leisure, take a long drag, then expostulate. He'd carry on in his smart-arse way about the aerodynamics of the thing, the engineering of the turbines and the astronomy of the navigation—the technology that can guide a jumbo jet from someplace to no place, a city at the bottom of the world, as if led by a magic lantern.

Then Danny'd drag again, blow a hoop with a click of his jaw, carry on about something else.

He was pretty smart, Danny. He was never happy until he'd pulled something apart, put it back together again, figured out what made it tick. They never worked him out at school. They asked the wrong questions. Which continent is Niger in? What assassination started World War I? What is the square root of sixteen? What is the symbol for hydrogen? All those worthless facts and figures. No wonder Danny failed. They asked the wrong questions.

'Don't piss on y'self!' Michelle calls.

Toby turns and, of course, pisses on his foot.

'Fuck.'

Michelle is tanning her overripe, freckled body on the banana lounge, long bleached-blonde hair flicked over the back of the chair so it doesn't stick to her skin, damp with perspiration.

Toby spins around, glimpses Michelle's breasts and looks away: half-annoyed, half-aroused. She never went topless before the accident.

'You're taking pictures,' Michelle laughs—pointing at his semi-erect penis with a painted finger.

Toby buttons himself up and walks over, blocking Michelle's sun.

'There's a dunny inside, y'know,' she says.

He stays put.

'You wanna move?'

'Nup.'

'Wrack off, Toby.'

Toby closes his eyes, sees Michelle stepping out of the Honda Civic again, sees himself waiting in the darkness again. He feels he has to do something, but doesn't know what.

Two

'Do you believe in ghosts?'

Danny turned serious when Toby asked him that question. The two of them were out in the backyard the week before the accident—Danny servicing his Yamaha, Toby watching.

Danny stopped working on the bike, turned round: 'What kinda ghosts?'

'Dunno. All kinds.'

'Why? D'you believe in 'em?'

'Dunno.'

'Have y'seen one?'

'Nup,' Toby said quickly.

Danny frowned, turned his attention back to the bike.

'I used to believe in 'em, but,' Toby volunteered. 'Y'know how Mum used to always be on the lookout? I thought she was looking for ghosts.'

Danny smiled: 'You like talking 'bout this shit, doncha?'

'Yeah.'

The two brothers stared at each other. Danny asked Toby to hand over the shifter: 'That one there, dopey, not the spanner. Ta.'

Toby watched his big brother work. Danny had a way about him, a physical ease and economy of movement, which, even when changing a spark plug, impressed and unsettled. Danny worked quickly, with surprising strength and stamina. Toby was struck by his brother's muscular grace and the knowledge that he could erupt at any moment, hammering a Torana's bent fender into an even more grotesque shape.

Danny finished with the spark plug and oil and tightened the chain; his hands working without pause. As he worked, sweat trickled down Danny's suede head, making the dark, exposed skin glisten. He wiped his hand across the base of his neck, leaving an oily smudge just above the knuckle of his spine.

Three

Danny's bike is not alive, not dead, but somewhere in between—laid out on the floor of the garage on a blue sheet of plastic, front wheel turned towards the roof. The wheel is buckled, the spokes twisted, the mirrors shattered, the chain broken, the cooling system bled dry, the frame scarred and fractured just below the steering head.

Danny never has accidents. Not ever. *Prangs*—that's what Danny has, that's his word. Like the time he went over the bonnet of an old geezer's Cortina in the Shoppingtown car park and broke his collarbone: that was a prang.

Danny had come home from the hospital, arm in a sling, wearing his leather jacket like a cape. Michelle was with him, eyes red from crying, but Danny was laughing, full of life.

'What a prang!' he announced as he came through the front door. 'Toby! What a prang! You shoulda seen it.'

Danny told Michelle to get him a beer, sat in the garage with Toby, describing the prang step-by-step: how the Cortina reversed out without looking, blocking the way; how Danny had nowhere to go, no time to stop; how he braked, hit the side of the sedan, went sailing over its bonnet; how, as he flew past the windshield, he saw the old geezer's mouth make a perfect O; how he mistimed his fall and landed on his shoulder. He took Toby through every aspect of the prang, again and again, like a fighter pilot in debriefing, until Toby felt as though he was there, a black-box recording in the back of Danny's head.

'What a prang,' Danny kept repeating.

Toby and Danny stayed out in the garage for hours, well into the night, sitting on old kitchen chairs with broken backs, drinking beer straight from the bottle.

'It was a trip—a fucken trip,' Danny said.

'Wish I'd been there,' Toby said.

'You shoulda seen it. I got up, real pissed off, and the old fart winds down his window, real polite, and goes, *Is there anything I can do?* So I go, Yeah. *Go fuck y'self.* So he just nods an' winds up his window. Sits there until the security guards come over. Scared shitless.'

'Then what happened?'

'Nuthin'. But I was charged up, ready to go.'

Toby gulped a mouthful of beer, asked Danny what he thought about.

Danny burped: 'What?'

'When you where fallin'. Did you think about anything? See anything?'

Danny stopped smiling: 'Don't be stupid.'

Michelle called out from the back step: 'Danny! I'm goin' to bed.'

'Hang on a tick!' Danny called back.

He skulled his stubby, leered at Toby: 'I'm charged up and ready to go.'

Toby sits on one of those backless kitchen chairs as the morning heat slowly builds inside the garage; peels out of his jeans, takes Danny's overalls off the peg and steps into them—is surprised to find them short in the leg. Toby has always thought himself smaller than his big brother. He kneels beside the Yamaha, fingers its metal skin, feels its scars, rummages through Danny's tool kit.

What should he start with? A screwdriver or a shifter or a hammer?

Four

Michelle spends ages in the bathroom, washing and painting herself, and surfaces just after midday—hair tizzed and moussed to within an inch of its life—wearing a backless summer dress and a face full of make-up.

'Got a job interview, have we? Lemme guess. Massage parlor,' Mum snarls.

Gran is sitting in the armchair across from Mum, rocking herself; forearms crossed—the palms of her hands cupping the points of her narrow shoulders.

Michelle glances at Gran, glares at Mum.

'I'll get a fucken job when Toby gets a fucken job.'

'He's been tryin'.'

'Tryin' what?'

Gran starts talking to the coffee table: 'Thank you. You're a splendid dancer too.'

'Shoosh, Gran,' says Mum.

'I come here once a year,' Gran smiles at the shadows.

'What's up with her?' Michelle motions with her head.

'Nuthin' a bullet wouldn't fix,' Mum mutters.

'But I dance every Saturday at the town hall,' Gran chimes in.

'Shit! Gran, shut up!' Mum bawls.

But Gran just beams: 'What did you say your name was?'

'She orright?'

'Jack, did you say?' Gran extends a hand. 'Hello Jack.'

'Old girl had a nervy turn last night. Look, Michelle, I wanna talk to you about Danny. Why haven't you gone to see him?'

Michelle folds her arms.

Mum softens: 'Look, I know he goes off the rails sometimes—y'know what I mean. But it's not all his fault'—an image rears in Michelle's mind as Mum speaks; Danny screaming at her, calling her 'slut', whipping her with an electric cord—'he's a good boy an' he loves you. He told me that, y'know—'

'Look,' Michelle says—cutting Mum off—'I have to go. I just have to, so can we do this later, please?' Michelle is desperate to get outside, into fresh air.

'Where y'going?' Mum asks.

'To see Cindy, a girl I used to work with at Safeway. She's had a baby.'

'Nice,' Mum says sarcastically.

'Dance? Why, Jack, I'd love to dance,' Gran starts humming a waltz and swaying in her seat.

'Fucken hell,' Mum growls.

'I've gotta see Cindy, she's sick, y'know,' Michelle says.

Michelle waves to Gran, pecks Mum on the cheek, hurtles out the front door, hustles around the corner, steps into a red Honda Civic.

Mum wipes off Michelle's kiss with the back of her hand. Gran is still jabbering away, telling everyone how hot she is from all this dancing. She is speaking in a giddy, girlish voice Mum has never heard before.

'So, you were young once?' Mum says, but Gran doesn't respond to her daughter. Wherever she's dancing, the music is too loud.

Gran talks so much she dribbles out of the corners of her mouth. Mum pulls a crumpled tissue from her sleeve, wipes Gran's mouth clean, sighs: 'I wish you'd just drop fucken dead.'

Five

Mum remembers being young. That was back when she had a name.

No one calls her Jacki now. Now she's Mum. Mum, when's dinner? Mum, where's my shirt? Mum, can I have some money? Mum, something's happened to Danny...

Falling pregnant with Danny changed everything. One day Jacki was a sixteen-year-old dreaming about—*what?* It was so long ago, that person so far gone, it was hard to picture what Jacki wanted from life. Travel? Excitement? Freedom?

Freedom. Young Jacki definitely wanted that—to be away from a long suffering mother and a father who hated her for breathing.

Pa called Jacki his tumour. Sometimes he yelled at Gran about having to feed and clothe the tumour. Then there was the time he lost a packet on the dogs, came home with a skinful and, while he punched Gran around the kitchen, kept bellowing that he was sick of paying for someone else's mistake. And Gran took it. Only cried if he hurt her badly.

Gran slapped Jacki if she asked about the things Pa said when he was drunk, but sat alone in the kitchen with the lights out late at night, smoking cigarette after cigarette. When she tottered down to the pub on a Saturday arvo to get tipsy on gin and beer, Gran didn't loosen up, either. She just quietened down. By the time she staggered home to slump on the couch and listen to the football or the races on the wireless she was as quiet as a mouse.

When Jacki got preggers, Gran and Pa finally had something to agree on. The girl was a slut, a tramp, a whore. Pa took to her with his belt. Gran slapped and scratched her face. The neighbours called the coppers. And Jacki spent the night in the lock-up.

The Senior Sergeant told Jacki she wasn't under arrest: 'Let's just give yer mum'n'dad time t'get used to the idea of being grandparents.'

But they didn't get used to it. Pa told Jacki that, as far as he was concerned, she now belonged to the man who knocked her up, Gary Nagle, so she better pack her bags. As for Gran, she just got the quiets, sat on the couch like it was Saturday arvo.

So Jacki left home.

And, when she called her mother on the phone, hysterical, and told her Gary had knocked out her front teeth, Gran replied, 'Big deal—teeth are a fucken luxury.'

And, when she turned up with the kids in the middle of the night—battered and bloodied—Gran just put the kettle on, dabbed around the corners with Dettol and cotton wool, settled Danny and Toby down, and called Gary. Jacki sat in Gran's kitchen, sipped tea through swollen lips, wished herself dead; Pa came out in his singlet and piss-stained Y-fronts, stared hard at Jacki, hated her on sight, wheeled round and went back to bed. And, next morning, riding home in the Falcon, she listened to Gary talk the same let's-make-a-happy-family bullshit.

On one of her late night visits, Jacki told Gran she didn't love Gary, she hated him.

Gran didn't twitch a muscle. Just slurped her tea.

'Who says a woman has to love a man?' she shrugged.

Six

Toby is perched on one of the old kitchen chairs.

Perspiration has soaked through the underarms and back of Danny's overalls, matted Toby's hair, smarted the corners of his eyes.

Lying before him along the far side of the plastic sheet, arranged from largest to smallest piece, is the bike's buckled front wheel, broken chain, warped spokes, and shattered mirror. In pieces.

The bike—lolled on its side—appears toothless without its wheel and, if anything, more broken down, more irredeemable, than ever before.

Seven

Suzie's working the front counter when Michelle blows in—head thrown back, laughing lightly at something Brendan said. Brendan runs a suntanned hand through his blow-dried hair, sucks in his gut as he ushers Michelle to a window seat. From here they can watch the traffic rush past, racing to and from the freeway which stops dead at Another. At the last possible moment, the freeway swings away from the hazard signs at the end of the line, a hard left funnelling into Another's main street, cutting a swathe through the raw subdivisions; passing McDonald's, the servo, a meagre shopping strip and giant LAND RUSH real estate billboards, before ploughing on, deeper, into an ocean of hard-baked grazing land.

Suzie keeps serving, keeping an eye on the happy couple.

Brendan bends over Michelle, whispers in her ear. One hand is flat on the table, the other resting on her bare shoulder.

Jenny comes over from the Drive-Thru window: 'Who's fatso fucking?'

Suzie raises a quizzical eyebrow.

'Lookit that,' Jenny hisses. 'He's perving at her tits.'

'Sunburnt tits.'

'Yeah. Not a good look under the fluoro lights.'

Brendan catches them staring, marches over.

'Thought you were out f'lunch,' Suzie says.

Brendan sniffs: 'And I thought you two worked for a living. Trays are still on half the tables and there's a cheeseburger on the floor.'

'Where?'

'Up front. Clean it up.'

'We've been busy.'

Brendan looks around the empty restaurant: 'Who with? The invisible man?'

'S'pose so.'

'And I suppose you two don't like working here, eh?'

Suzie says, 'Suppose we,' but Jenny grabs her arm before she utters *don't*.

The veins on Brendan's forehead bulge: 'What was that?'

'We do,' Jenny interprets. 'We suppose we do.'

Suzie stares blankly.

'Yeah, right,' Brendan says and leans over the counter, locking his elbows.

He drops his voice: 'I know someone's been giving out free burgers.'

Jenny blinks.

'Yeah,' Brendan continues. 'Free burgers. That's stealing, eh, and I know all about it cos I've been keeping a bun tally. I'm right onto it. And when I find out who's been stealing they're history. I'll call in the cops.'

Jenny manages an 'oh'.

Brendan tries to shift from intimidation to inspiration: 'Y'know girls, we're doing something important here. This is the most remote McDonald's in the metropolitan area. People are moving out here to build a new suburb and we're feeding those people—and that's important. Now everyone else here realizes this, but not you two...Now I want two Big Mac Meal Deals on the double.'

Toby props against the ORDER HERE box—says, 'Hullo.'

'Toby?' the fibreglass contraption squawks, then whispers, 'Suzie, come here.'

'Jenny? Hullo?'

The box hisses.

'Jenny?'

'No,' the box squawks, 'It's me.'

'Suzie.'

'What're y'doin' here?'

Toby smiles: 'Quarterpoundermealdeal.'

'Toby.'

'Quarterpoundermealdeal.'

'I can't.'

'Quarterpounder—'

'Fuck off.'

'—mealdeal...Suzie.'

The box hisses static.

'I'm thirsty, Suzie.'

"There's a tap out back. Bye.'

Disgruntled, Toby stalks towards the side door—but stops short.

Michelle is sitting at the window with Brendan. Toby sees Michelle's sunburnt back, elbows planted on the laminate table-top, as she tucks into a Big Mac; sees Brendan talking and chewing, thoroughly engrossed in himself; sees Jenny mopping up a mangled cheeseburger. Suzie is nowhere to be seen. Probably at the Drive-Thru window, Toby thinks. He walks around the back of the building, douses his head under the tap, which runs warm, then lukewarm, until, finally, cold water pumps through its baked pipes, cooling his skull. He suckles on the tap, feeding greedily on the water, which spills down his chin and chest, drenching the front of Danny's overalls, only stopping when his gullet is swollen with water.

Sitting on the bitumen, eyes closed, leaning against the wall, Toby lets the heat lick him dry. It prickles—tightening his skin, baking his hair until it is hot to touch, turning the soaked fabric of the overalls into canvas. He sits there until he starts to sweat again, then opens his eyes—notices the Honda Civic sitting across the car park, blind headlights staring straight through him.

Prick, Toby thinks, Prob'ly has air conditioning. Maybe even a CD player... He scans the vicinity. Clear.

He circles the Civic. No alarm.

He tries the driver's door. Locked.

He tries the passenger door. It clicks open.

Toby smiles.

Eight

Another day burns itself across the sky—scorching the phosphorous earth, heating charcoal roads, igniting the air.

Here there is little shade.

The tall trees have long gone: carved into railway sleepers, fence posts, out-dated newspapers, wood chip, chewed pencils, the skeleton frames of so many three-bedroom habitations.

Gone, too, is the eucalyptus scent, the cool shade, the living history.

The sun is at its peak...pygmy saplings offer no respite...car interiors become pressure-cookers, blow engine hoses...crucifix shadows of 747s, passing overhead, flicker across the earth...high-voltage pylons throw deformed, stick-figure shadows...row after row of houses offer only umbrellas of shade beneath patios and verandahs...air-conditioners kick into high gear...ceiling fans click on...ice-trays are emptied...

And the day stretches: drowsy; rudderless.

I see fire.

Men in orange overalls, gloves, boots and helmets are burning off dead grass and thistle beside Another's main road.

In their intensity the flames are rendered almost invisible, consuming the dead grass, converting the grass into fuel, rearing up, taller than a man, radiating enough heat to warp the air, starting spot fires closer to the road, pressing against the line of men, only to be beaten back by fire extinguishers.

I see the flames along the roadside. Beaten back, they burn low, bide their time as cars and trucks pass; hypnotic in their languid beauty.

A wind kicks up, blowing away from the road, away from the men, towards the houses. And in an instant the fire rears up, hurdles a drainage ditch. It has mounted the nature-strip by the time the men catch it, containing it with their fire extinguishers.

Cars slow, drive through the haze of smoke as the firefighters corral, then kill, the runaway fire, leaving black stubble that will smoulder all afternoon and well into the evening.

Nine

Through the front window, Suzie sees smoke blown from further up the main road. Behind her, beef patties sizzle on the grill.

'Do you think she likes him?' Jenny asks.

Brendan leans back, talks expansively; Michelle, still propped forward on her elbows, nods and smiles.

'Couldn't give a shit,' Suzie replies. 'I hope they both get food poisoning an' die of constipation...Did he pay for those Big Macs?'

'Course not.'

'Typical.'

'D'you think he knows about Toby?'

'What about Toby?'

'The freebies—he reckons he's been keeping a bun tally.'

'Brendan's a wanker.'

Arm in arm, Brendan and Michelle head for the exit.

'Clean up girls,' Brendan commands.

'Prick!' Jenny yells once the door closes behind Brendan.

'That's telling him,' Suzie sneers as she picks up the trays.

Jenny turns peevish: 'That Brendan. He's such a—'

'—prick. I know, orright?'

'Orright. So, where'd Toby go?'

Suzie shrugs, sponges down the table.

'He's gunna have to start paying for his Quarter Pounders, y'know.'

Suzie is about to tell Jenny to piss off when Brendan bursts back through the door, frantic.

'What's wrong now?' Suzie asks in her most woe betide tone.

'Shit!' Brendan yells.

'What?' Jenny screws up her nose.

That's when Suzie notices Brendan's wet slacks—and starts laughing. She laughs so hard she drops her tray; she laughs so hard she has to sit down on a fibreglass swivel chair.

Ten

Finally the sun subsides.

Darkness approaches.

At night the shadows unfurl from their hiding places—travelling beneath the oily bellies of station wagons and sedans—stretching out along the long shadows of the high-voltage pylons—pressing flat against the cool sides of houses.

Some shadows take the shape of arms and legs, black-eyed faces, beak and wing, the tiger snake in the long grass.

Others have no design. They swell and contract—depending on the breeze—float down streets, pass through houses; make people rant and rave.

If you breathe the shadows into your lungs they mix with blood, flow into the heart, are pumped around the body, infect the tissue of the brain.

One tribe of shadows haunts Another—searching for dead fathers, raped mothers, stolen children—the shadows of the people who belonged to the land—the shadows of the people who mistook the white invaders for ghosts—the shadows of the people who discovered that the invaders were not ghosts but ghost-makers. Floating about the estate, the shadows throw sparks whenever they pass through electric fences.

Eleven

For once, Gran's sitting up at the table—and she is not happy. Mum's wedged her chair between the wall and the edge of the table to keep her from wriggling free, but still has to drum her spoon on the kitchen table, make choo-choo-choo noises, to drag her attention away from the TV which has been blaring ever since Toby came back from McDonald's. As soon as Gran's head turns Mum's way—*Bingo!*—another spoonful is shovelled into her mouth. Half-chewed potatoes and vegetables are sprayed across the tabletop.

'That's right. Chew. Good,' Mum says. 'What's got into you t'day?'

Gran has been stroppy all day, ever since Mum unlocked her bedroom door. Gran'd wet the bed so Mum strips off her soaked nightie and marches her into the bathroom, runs a bath. Gran stands up in the bath, ranting and raving, and refusing to part with her blue beanie. So Mum lets Gran wear the beanie and scrubs and sponges the rest of her scrawny body. It takes an hour to get Gran cleaned and dried and dressed. Finally Mum props her in front of the telly and goes back to her bedroom, which smells like cat piss.

As Mum strips the bed, Michelle passes the open doorway.

'Hey!' Mum calls.

Michelle stops in the corridor, hovers.

'Gimme a hand with the mattress. It needs to dry.'

'Later,' Michelle replies. 'I need a shower.'

Of course, there isn't a later. Michelle shuts herself in the bathroom until past midday, then comes out wearing a truckload of make-up, talking about visiting some girlfriend with a newborn baby.

Must be a baby boom out here, Mum thinks.

So Mum ends up dragging Gran's stained mattress outside by herself, props it against the fence to dry, washes Gran's sheets and hangs them on the line, goes back inside and perches on the couch beside Gran.

Gran is engrossed in the telly, which is playing a rerun of *Perry Mason*, but she turns to her daughter, looks her steadily in the eye.

'What's on telly?' Mum asks.

'I shouldn't have blamed you,' Gran sighs.

'What? Blamed me for what?'

'For everything,' Gran says—then turns back to the telly, mouths an advertising jingle for an airline.

Gran loves jingles. Now the nightly news anthem plays—an urgent burst of brass instruments—and she's hooked: stops chewing, spits out her food, spills a glass of prune juice as she tries to upend the kitchen table.

'Shit-a-brick,' Mum says.

Gran slips and catches her chin on the table.

'Toby!' Mum calls.

'What?' he calls back.

'Turn that thing off. The racket's driving Gran bonkers.'

'She's already bonkers.'

'Turn it down!'

'I'm watching somethin'.'

'An' I'm trying to feed Gran.'

'So?'

'Jeez! Where's Michelle?'

'Giving some bloke a head-job, prob'ly.'

'Toby! Get out!'

Toby stands and boots the TV—bouncing it against the wall and onto the floor, where it expires in a shower of sparks—before storming out the front door.

Twelve

The horizon swallows the sun—setting off a glow of yellow, orange, and red—always red.

Cars click on headlights, streetlights flicker into life, houses shutter their venetian blinds and close curtains, children are called in off the streets, and, gradually, shadows unwind from the still-warm earth.

The shadow beneath the caravan rises—forming the long barrel of a rifle—a hand to hold the rifle—an eye to sight the rifle—then another hand to squeeze the trigger.

Thirteen

Mum's still trying to coax the telly back to life, with Gran watching hopefully from the couch, when Michelle bursts through the front door; hammers it shut so hard it springs open again.

'Steady,' Mum says.

'Shove it,' Michelle calls back as she flounces off to her bedroom.

Another door slams.

'Is the telly orright?' Gran asks.

'Hang on,' Mum sighs. She gets up and goes and knocks on Michelle's bedroom door.

'What?' asks Michelle's exasperated voice from behind the door.

'What's up?'

The door is flung open and Michelle pushes past, stripped down to her undies and bra, dress screwed in a ball.

'Michelle?'

Mum follows her to the laundry. Michelle fills the basin, scrunches the dress into the water.

'What happened?'

'Toby did it.'

Mum smells the urine: 'Toby peed on you?'

Michelle pushes past again and heads for the bathroom.

Mum follows.

'Michelle. You sure Gran didn't do it?'

Michelle runs the shower, steps out of her undies, unclips her bra, glares at Mum.

'I've had enough of this fucken joint. Now can I please have some privacy?'

She shoves Mum in the chest—slams the door in her face.

Fourteen

A flood of shadows sweep along the back fences—rise from the water table. Toby is caught in a stream of shadows—colour, heat, and disjointed shapes—as those shadows of a once great river roll through Another, flowing inland. He feels the force at his back and goes with it, swimming fast to keep his head above the surface.

He is running—sprinting along the back fences.

To stop running would be to lose the reason for running. To stop running would be to lose the momentum of the shadows.

So Toby runs—swept along with the shadow river.

He runs until he is gasping for air, lungs on fire, swallowing shadow water to put out that fire. He runs and runs and runs.

He runs until, exhausted, he collapses in the dirt with a mouth full of clag.

Toby is drenched.

Danny's overalls cling to him. He doubles over, head in hands, fighting for breath—stays that way until the fire in his lungs is reduced to embers.

Finding his feet, Toby trudges upstream against the shadow tide. Passing by a back fence, he hears laughter. Music. A woman's voice. Then a man's.

Curious, he pulls himself up the back fence with a chin-up, braces his weight by laying his arms across the top of the fence—cannot believe what he sees.

A man and a woman are simmering in an outdoor spa beneath the stars, starkers.

Their champagne flutes are grubby with sweaty fingerprints and the carbonated dregs of two empty bottles of champagne, both of which now bob in the in-ground pool. Pink lipstick is frosted around the rim of one flute.

To Toby this is a manifestation of outer-suburban utopia.

The man is well into middle age. Overweight, bald and grey, grimacing as he wrestles with the cork of a third bottle of champagne, trying to shoot it into space.

The woman, a young plump blonde, is laughing coquettishly—massaging his sternum with the ball of her foot.

With a pop, the cork is fired into the night sky and the woman lets out a 'wheeee!' Claps her hands extravagantly. She grabs her champagne glass, holds it out, but, instead of filling her glass, the man holds the frothing bottle in his right hand, mouth ajar, as he watches the cork's majestic ascent. The cork slows gradually as it valiantly tries to throw off Earth's gravitational pull, enter orbit. Its trajectory arcs, peaks—momentarily attaining weightlessness before descending, completing a perfect parabola as it performs a splashdown in the pool. Only then does the man refill the woman's empty flute.

Fifteen

Michelle's ready to go. The suitcase is crammed with her clothes, shoes and hair-drier. One plastic shopping bag is stacked with make-up and magazines, another quarantines the soggy floral dress. She's perched on the corner of the bed, which is stripped clean, while lacing up her old Reeboks.

Mum barges in: 'What're you doing?'

'Leaving.'

'You can't be serious.'

'I can,' Michelle's voice is quiet, firm.

'But you can't be leaving.'

'I am.'

Mum folds her arms, breaks her taboo: 'Whaddabout Danny?'

'I'm sorry about Danny.'

'Sorry? You're just pissing off. You've leeched us dry so you're pissing off.'

'You've been telling me to get out—now I am, an' you're telling me to stay.'

'I've been telling you t'get a job.'

'An' I've been trying to get one.'

'Crap.'

'I'm leaving.'

Mum plants her hands on her hips: 'Well, if you're goin' you can't take that suitcase.'

'Why?'

'Cos it's mine.'

'But you gave it to me.'

Michelle was given the suitcase by Mum as a sort-of-wedding present, even though she and Danny never did get around to being officially married—just bought the ring and had the honeymoon.

'It's mine. It's not meant to leave this house.'

'Well, it is now.'

Michelle tries to get by Mum, into the hallway.

'Look, Mum, I've gotta go. I don't have time for this.'

'Where're you going?'

'I'm goin' to stay with a friend, orright? I'm goin' an' you can't stop me this time. I'm goin' if I have to carry my stuff outta here in a rubbish bag.'

'Who're you gunna stay with? This Cindy girl?'

'A friend.'

'Who?!'

'Not Danny! Orright? Not Danny!'

The words punch Mum in the face. Her shoulders sag.

Michelle softens: 'Look, Mum, it's not you, it's not Gran—it's not even Toby. It's just that I gotta go.'

'I can...we can give you more room...I'll talk to Toby an' you won't have to worry about Gran. She's my problem.'

'No, Mum. No.'

Mum sits on the carpet, defeated: 'So you're leaving us? Leaving Danny?'

'I gotta go.'

'Why? Why've you gotta go?'

Michelle chews a fingernail: 'Y'know, Mum, you've been sitting round waiting for Gran to die. Me? I'm sick of waiting...'

Mum presses the issue: 'If this is about how Danny treated you sometimes...well, I know he's no saint—'

So why didn't you stop him? thinks Michelle.

'But you still love him, don't you?' Mum continues.

'None of that matters anymore.'

'It's this family, isn't it? They can't help themselves. One father beats it into his son an' then that son beats it into his next son...I tried to escape it, get Danny away from it—he was a good boy, too. But that bastard hunted me down. Hunted me down like a fucken dog...'

Mum is crying. Abandoned to memories of seeing Gary in the supermarket, waiting for him with a knife from the dresser—then the fire.

Mum ploughs on: 'What is it with men? What is it with them? They only ever want to fuck or fight. Even Danny...Jeez, he was such a beautiful boy....'

Michelle rubs the faint white scar on the back of her right hand.

Sixteen

Headlights flare across Michelle's bedroom window as a car pulls into the drive with its horn honking.

'That's my lift,' Michelle says.

Mum picks herself up from the carpet: 'Orright.'

Michelle gathers the suitcase and shopping bags, heads for the front door where she pauses.

The two women lock eyes.

Mum takes a step towards Michelle, then stops, folds her arms—nods as though granting permission for takeoff.

Michelle nods back, walks down the steps onto the gravel drive into the white glare of the car's headlights.

Driving away, Michelle sticks her elbow out the window, wonders whether she's making another mistake. Another Danny.

Seventeen

Michelle met Danny at the Shoppingtown Nightclub.

It was a Friday night. She changed in the toilets after work at Safeway and—*Presto!*—emerged transformed: a butterfly in a little black dress. She sashayed over to the shopping centre lift and took it to the top floor, the Shoppingtown Nightclub where boys and girls drank, smoked, danced, and pouted at each other, pretending they were actors in some Hollywood movie. Michelle ascended the elevator shaft in that little black dress of hers, black butterfly wings folded beneath her shoulder blades, and danced with her handbag on the floor between her feet. Cigarette in one hand, rum-and-Coke in the other, she sang the words to her favourite songs. Michelle, Kelly, Cindy, and Josephine—all the Friday night checkout chicks—were there and dressed to kill: pancake makeup, stiletto heels, electrocuted hair, false nails, big smiles.

Michelle's body was warm—lubricated with alcohol and nicotine. She floated above the dance floor. Kelly and Cindy were dancing with her. Josephine minded their table. Prince, Madonna and George Michael were playing and barely any of the boys were dancing. Instead, they lined the walls, crowded the bar, watched the girls dance, waited for the DJ to play something by Eminem or a classic Guns'n'Roses tune. Cindy danced over to Michelle—smiling broadly—yelled 'Someone likes you!' in her ear.

Michelle mouthed, 'Who?'

Cindy pointed over her shoulder with her ciggie.

And there was Danny—in bikie boots and black leather jacket—nursing a rum-and-Coke, staring straight at her. His unblinking gaze made her turn away, glance back again. Cindy nudged Michelle. Kelly yelled 'Go! Go! Go girl!' with a faux-American accent.

The opening guitar line of "Welcome to the Jungle" came on, sweet as a bell, bringing packs of boys tumbling onto the floor, swaying and rocking like so many pretend Axl Roses. Michelle, Cindy, and Kelly picked up their handbags from the floor and strutted over to Josephine at their table. By the time Michelle sat down, Danny was at her elbow.

'Watcha drinking?' he asked.

When Michelle said 'Rum'n'Coke', Danny lifted his plastic cup.

'Me, too,' he said, 'We're a perfect match.'

Danny introduced himself, finished off every second sentence with 'Jeez, you're so fucken beautiful,' bought Michelle a string of rum-and-Cokes, offered her a joint, even danced with her to a George Michael song. He was intense, this Danny boy—he never stopped staring at Michelle, barely blinked, smiled just the once, showing his chipped front teeth. Michelle liked the fact that he liked her, gave her his undivided attention, not chattering or showing off. She wasn't so sure about the intensity of his unwavering gaze.

'Whadda you want?' he asked at one stage.

Michelle sipped her drink, confessed, 'A big wedding,' then giggled with embarrassment.

Danny didn't blink, didn't smile.

'How big?' he asked.

'Big cake, big dress, big hair. Big everything!'

Danny skulled the rest of his rum-and-Coke, dragged on his joint, slit his eyes.

'I can live with that,' he finally pronounced.

Michelle and Danny carried on for hours, brushing up against each other. Josephine grew bored and went home. Kelly left with her boyfriend. Finally, Cindy rattled her keys wearily in Michelle's face.

'I'm leaving!' Cindy yelled. 'Comin'?'

Michelle was perched on Danny's lap by now. She shook her head. She was staying.

Next weekend, Danny dinked Michelle down to a beach caravan park, slipped a gold band onto her ring finger. They both said 'I do' and popped a bottle of cheap champagne on the beach.

'As good as married,' Michelle said.

'Better than married,' Danny replied. 'We don't need the piece of paper.'

'I'd like a wedding, but.'

'Oh, yeah—as soon as I get some cash together.'

So Danny moved out of the caravan, commandeered Toby's bedroom, borrowed Mum's double bed—and Michelle moved in. And they were happy for a while.

Danny worked at the panel-beater's as an apprentice, Michelle worked at Safeway as a checkout chick. They opened a joint bank account and talked about buying a block of land, building a house. Danny even came home one night sporting a tattoo on his right biceps—*Michelle*—printed in black across a flaming red heart. And, every Friday night they returned to the nightclub, where Danny drank by himself and Michelle danced by herself.

'Can you smell it?' Brendan is upset.

Michelle shakes her head, stares out the passenger window as Another rushes past.

Brendan slaps the steering wheel: 'I can smell it.'

The interior of the car reeks of air-freshener. The floral scent makes Michelle's eyes water. Heavy-duty plastic bags are spread over the seats.

'Shit. I'll have to get the seats shampooed.'

Michelle pulls out a cigarette.

'Do you have to?'

'What?'

'Smoke—d'you mind?'

'The window's open.'

'You'll stink out the car.'

'It already stinks.'

Michelle pushes on the Honda's cigarette lighter, but Brendan pops it out. She pushes it in again and he pops it out again. The tug-of-war continues until Brendan wrenches the lighter from its socket and tosses it onto the back seat.

'If you wanna smoke go buy your own car,' he says.

Big mistake, Michelle thinks.

Darkness

One

I am sleeping. I am dreaming. I am reaching out for Suzie. Searching for Suzie.

But I cannot find her.

I have no images of Suzie.

Just sensations. The rush of another's blood through my veins, the muscular embrace of the womb. The asphyxiating fog of cigarette smoke and carbon monoxide—the residual of so many combustion engines idling in the heat—lightens my head, makes me rotate clockwise, frog-kick in the womb.

Just sounds. A double beat underpinning a dislocated train of thought; Suzie's mental arithmetic.

She is thinking: A hundred dollars.

She is running calculations: A hundred dollars is sixty-seven dollars after tax. A hundred dollars is ten casks of white wine. A hundred dollars is ten packs of cigarettes. A hundred dollars is fifty individually wrapped cigars. A hundred dollars is a new pair of black jeans. A hundred dollars is a ticket to see Kylie in concert. A hundred dollars is a night in a three-star hotel. A hundred dollars is two shifts flipping burgers and frying fries in a fast-food restaurant. A hundred dollars is Ecstasy.

A hundred dollars is a lot of money for Suzie to find.

Two

This sunken corner of Another, once a swimming hole, is now a maze of shadows and ghosts: the shadows of giant gum trees; the ghosts of black children.

The ghosts relive their stories...the ghost-makers poisoning the water...the bodies of so many children floating, face down...wailing mothers and fathers wading into the water...a still, deadly place—abandoned...a dumping ground foul with death...

The water is gone now, pumped away, leaving a dry hollow, thistle and generations of refuse—the sunken ground laced with heavy metals and the forgotten skeletons of poisoned children.

Old Hanlon had this land rezoned after his first subdivision sold so quickly, but has been disappointed. The subdivisions sat. Did not sell. Went stale.

The asking price was cut but the subdivisions still barely moved. Buyers didn't like the location—didn't like the fact that, in a flood, these subdivisions were the first underwater, the last to drain. The more diligent agents still worked the subdivision hard—driving clients, usually young married couples with just enough money to make a five per cent deposit, out in their air-conditioned Falcons. The agents took the value-for-money angle with the husbands: 'Buying off the plan saves stamp duty, and that's big dollars. And investing in the cheapest land is a smart investment because the value can only ever go up, and that's a financial fact.' Then swung over to the safety angle for the wives: 'Crime is not an issue out here. It's a clean, safe place to raise kids.'

But, no matter which way the agents tacked, the success-rate of the spiel was poor. Most people saw through the bullshit or became unsettled after a walk down through the dust and thistles—sensing something untoward beneath their shoes. There have been buyers, though—people who cannot afford to look elsewhere. Slowly but surely, subdivisions have been sold, homes built. These are the homes of the naive and the desperate.

There are no fences, no streetlights, to be found at this end of the estate. Just a calamity of subdivisions: unsold subdivisions, empty subdivisions with SOLD signs, subdivisions with concrete foundations, subdivisions with skeleton wooden frames, subdivisions with the shells of just-built houses (plastic still covering their windows), and subdivisions with finished houses—complete with electricity, sewerage, occupants, and a car in the drive. This is a neighborhood in the early stages of evolution, caught somewhere between the amoebae and the mudfish.

Toby likes it here. Here he can walk, invisible in the darkness, and lie flat out on those concrete foundations; wander through the skeleton houses, smell the rough timber, try to imagine which room will be which; walk right up to the new houses without fences or curtains and look inside—see everything.

A new house, in Monaro Crescent, sits on its own. No fences. No dog. No neighbours. Just dirt, thistles, and brazen real estate signs.

The outside light is on, but the driveway is empty.

...Toby circles the house (all the rooms are dark)...rings the doorbell (nobody answers)...tries the front door (locked)...tries the windows (locked)...tries the backdoor (locked)...

Fuck, he thinks. There's gotta be a key here.

He checks under the mat...in the water meter...beside the gully trap...under a pot plant: nothing.

Where is it?

There: standing on the brick path beside the clothes-line, smirking at him. A garden gnome wearing a red hat. Toby grabs the gnome by its hat, shakes, something rattles inside. He shakes the gnome by its pointy head, trying to coax it to relinquish its hold. The gnome's red hat slips from his greasy hands and...*PINKRIIIISH!!*...there is a ceramic explosion as the gnome hits the bricks.

Toby drops to his knees. Freezes. Waits...but nothing happens.

There is no one around. No one to call the police. The shattered gnome smiles up at Toby from the paving.

'Dickhead,' Toby whispers, fingers through the gnome's remains until he touches something metallic. A key. It fits snugly into the deadlock, clicks open the back door.

Inside, the heat hits Toby in the face.

The house has been shut up all afternoon, baking in the sun. Toby fumbles for the switch, clicks on the lights, waits until his eyes adjust.

First impressions are not good. There isn't a drier or even a washing machine in the laundry—just white towels soaking in a green plastic bucket on the floor. The kitchen is bare. An electric jug and toaster sit on the bench, dirty dishes in the sink: a cardboard box in the corner has been converted into a makeshift rubbish bin. There are no pictures for the walls, no stools for the breakfast bench, no chairs or table for the dining area.

The lounge room is worse. Two director's chairs sit in the very centre of a bare room beneath a naked light bulb with only a portable TV for company. The portable's cord snakes across the apricot carpet and plugs into the white wall. There is no other furniture in the room. The spartan chairs and portable are surrounded by a large rectangle of carpet so new it still emits little balls of apricot nylon fluff whenever it is walked over. A pair of women's slip-on shoes lie where they were kicked off, beside the chairs.

There are no curtains in the room. This realization—that he is standing in the barren lounge, lit up like a Christmas tree—leaves Toby feeling terribly exposed. He hurries to the bedrooms.

The main bedroom is at the front of the house: an unmade futon is pushed against the far wall, clothes are dumped unceremoniously about the floor. A grey blanket with a pale purple check pattern hangs over the window, acting as a makeshift curtain. A gold chain coiled on top of the clock-radio catches Toby's eye. He pockets the chain and goes out to the hall.

Something is wrong here. Toby cannot overcome the feeling that something is amiss. Perhaps it is the air—so stale and synthetic, like a new car left out in the sun. Perhaps it is the unfinished nature of the house—barely furnished, no light fittings, ragged holes where power points should be—and the dearth of doors. Hinges have been drilled onto the jambs, but no doors attached; not for the bedrooms, not for the lounge room, not even for the toilet.

Toby clicks on the bathroom and toilet lights, finds nothing of interest, and heads for the second bedroom. Cardboard boxes are stacked on top of each other around the walls, books piled on the floor; Toby slags on the apricot carpet and heads for the third bedroom at the end of the hall. Something is whirring inside the room: a gust of warm air blows across Toby's face, stops him dead in the doorway.

A fan.

Toby stands still until the electric fan arcs back across his face again. He turns on the light, but immediately clicks it off.

Shit.

Toby stands perfectly still, listening to his beating heart. He wants to run, but cannot.

It's awake.

Toby saw its blue eyes when he clicked on the light.

Shit-a-brick.

Slowly, Toby's eyes adjust to the dark...he walks in from the doorway...stands beside the bassinet...gazes down at the baby.

Is it a boy or a girl?

The baby is half-awake, half-dreaming. Her eyes no longer blue, now black. She has drifted in and out of sleep—sometimes mistaking the stifling heat of this room for the womb—sometimes forgetting to breathe, letting her heartbeat slow almost to stalling before waking.

Now her eyes flash. Flash black. Flash blue. Flash black again—and her heart resumes its beating.

The baby thinks—as I do—in a liquid language of colour. But the language is fading—slowly being replaced by concrete thoughts ('Say Daddaddaddaddad!') that will soon be spoken as concrete words.

And when she sleeps she still sees the images—dislocations of past, present, and future—but those, too, are being overrun by the circus images and flashing lights of the world. As the baby's eyes adjust, bringing the world into focus, the dream images fade.

The baby knows someone is in the room—can feel Toby's beating heart. She tunes her heart to beat in unison—feels the tom-tom of his heart and no longer knows whether she is awake or dreaming: in the bassinet or in the womb.

The baby kicks—making my own toy heart surge—so I kick, too.

Toby is compelled to run, compelled to stay.

He gazes down at the baby—a baby with an Asian face, European eyes—and finds himself touching the child, brushing her cheek with his hand. Then he is running. Out the front door, down the steps, into the darkness—leaving all the lights blazing.

Three

Sal hears a *beepbeep! beepbeep!* noise and drops flat, hitting the bitumen with the rim of his spray-can in the process, making a metallic racket, giving himself away. A stream of panicked obscenities pound through his rodent brain. He badly wants to pee. Lying there, face pressed against the car park, he wishes his brother—or anyone—was with him so he didn't have to be alone, scurrying about the periphery: a living ghost with a spray-can. But then Sal gets riled. Starts swearing—calling himself a gutless poofter, imagining people laughing at him, pointing at him.

'Fuckers,' Sal whispers and jumps to his feet.

His head pinballs around—but just sees another mum and dad taking their kids into McDonald's and a queue of cars at the Drive-Thru. He finishes spraying NO NIPS on the tailgate of a station-wagon, then walks away briskly, shaking his spray can absently in his hand so that it clickclickclicks nervously as he walks along the line of parked cars, keeping his head turned towards the restaurant. But a voice hisses in the darkness—says 'Sal'—and Sal is flat against the bitumen again, on the verge of pissing his pants again.

Four

Suzie.

As soon as I hear her call to Sal, my toy heart expands. I kick.

Suzie.

Her name soothes me. Her voice sings to me. Her body nurtures me.

Soo-zee.

Can she feel me? I try to call out but my lungs fill with amniotic fluid.

(Suzie.)

You are the sun I orbit around.

Suzie calls to Sal again.

'Over here,' she says.

Sal scrambles to his feet, scampers over to an empty parking bay, finds Suzie sitting cross-legged in her McDonald's uniform, smoking her last cigarette.

'Hi, Sal,' Suzie says.

'Hi,' Sal says, 'I gotta piss.'

'Do it downhill from me, orright?'

'Yeah,' Sal smiles and walks over to a Nissan Pulsar.

Suzie stays put in her parking bay, squinting at the servo. Jenny and some kids she used to go to school with are hanging around, talking, smoking, watching a primary school kid with baggy pants and a Chicago Bulls singlet muck about inexpertly on a skateboard.

Sal comes back, wiping his hands on his jeans.

'Whadda you doin'?' he asks.

'I'm sittin'. Whadda you doin'?' she counters.

Sal props on one leg, rattles his head: 'Nuthin'.'

'Yeah.'

He edges close: 'Can I, you know, can I have a brew?'

'Nup. This is my last one.'

'Oh.'

Sal starts to drift away.

'Sal?'

He stops drifting.

'Whadda you doin'?'

'D'you really wanna know?'

She throws up both hands as if to say, *Of course.*

'Orright,' Sal says, getting excited, 'I gotta fucken brilliant idea.'

Having smoked that last sweet cigarette down to the filter, Suzie flicks it to the bitumen, lets it glow.

'What idea?' she asks.

'Mobile Graffiti,' he pronounces the words as though they were patented.

'Mobile what?'

'Graffiti. I'm sick of spray painting walls an' shit. If I spray paint a car, but, when it drives round, everyone sees m'graffiti, eh? Get it?'

'You're spray-painting cars?'

'Yep.'

'An' whadda you sayin'?'

'What?'

'On the cars. Whadda you sayin'?'

Sal ponders the question: 'Depends how big the car is.'

Five

Suzie's mind is a mantra: a hundred dollars, a hundred dollars, a hundred dollars.

Without a cigarette to hold, she plays with her hands—cracking her knuckles one by one, chewing her stunted nails, running her fingers through her hair—not knowing where to put them—wishing she could chop them off just above the wrist, pop them in a clear plastic bag that seals shut at the top; keep them out of mischief.

Sal has gone off into the shadows—spray painting No Nips on the side of a shiny Tarago van—and Suzie is not sure how to behave when alone. She pinches herself: feels nothing.

Suzie imagines her skin is like the car park bitumen: a black husk, set hard and fast, baked and cracked by the sun; needing a jack-hammer to break through, into living flesh. She pulls out her velcro wallet. A rectangle of neatly folded white tissue paper is wedged in a pocket where a credit card or a driver's license should be. The tissue paper unfolds in Suzie's hand—a paper flower—uncovering a razor blade so thin it flexes when pinched between thumb and index finger. Suzie breathes on one side of the razor, polishes it with a corner of the tissue; turns the blade over, repeats the process.

The razor ready, Suzie licks the milk skin on the inside of her forearm, from her elbow down to her wrist, until it is slick with saliva, she scrapes the blade across the soft inside of her left forearm—teases herself.

Six

Toby cannot stop running. He is breathless—ragged—filthy with oil, sweat, and dust as he breaks away from the shadows, enters the penumbra of the car park lights, slows to a jog, makes a beeline for the servo.

Still dressed in her McDonald's uniform, Jenny is leaning against the glass wall of the servo. Her boyfriend, Matt, is sitting on the concrete.

'Good one,' Jenny says as Toby jogs up to them.

Toby stops, doubles over to catch his breath. 'Good what?'

'You know.'

'No, I don't.'

'Oh, yeah.'

Toby glances at Matt, who bristles. He is solid, Matt is, an impressive slab of fat and muscle and piggy eyes. Solid but slow. Toby wishes he were Danny—because then he'd hurt Matt. Knee him in the balls. Kick him into a crack in the wall.

'Seen Suzie?' he asks with unintended urgency.

Jenny holds up her hand like a traffic cop: 'I'm not talking to you.'

'Where's Suzie?'

'You're such an arse-hole. All you care about is feedin' y'face.'

Toby's voice drops: 'Where is she?'

'You right?' Matt asks Toby—the two of them standing close enough to kiss.

Toby transfers his weight from his heels to the balls of his feet, remembers the sound of Lionel Blackmore's head cracking the asphalt.

Jenny steps between the two of them.

'Back in your box,' she tells Matt.

'Prick,' Matt growls at Toby.

'Cunt,' Toby shoots back.

Jenny shoves Matt aside: 'Piss off. I can handle this.'

She turns on Toby: 'And you. You nearly got me the fucken sack, y'know.'

'How?'
'Oh, you know.'
'Where's Suzie? Tell me.'
Jenny points towards the car park.
'Ta,' he says and runs off.
'Fucken prick,' Matt hisses after him.

Seven

Headlights can only illuminate what lies ahead, can only lead away from Danny. Michelle toys with the side mirror so she can see what's following. She feels as though she is running away. She feels as though she is being pursued. She expects to see the headlight of Danny's bike, a single shining orb, appear in her mirror, loom larger and larger like an oncoming comet. She leans close to the mirror, the wind whipping through the window makes her eyes tear as the car turns off the freeway, starts ducking through the suburban streets—a maze of neat lawns, mail boxes, brown and red brick houses, and terracotta roofs. Watching the headlights pan across the blank brick veneer faces of countless houses, making windows glint, Michelle thinks of the mirror-ball at the Shoppingtown Nightclub—twinkling above the dance-floor as the spotlight refracts off its many faces.

Danny should've let me go dancing with my girlfriends, she tells herself.

Danny turned up at Shoppingtown Nightclub every Friday. He refused to dance but watched his de facto dance—sullen, brooding. He told Michelle he just couldn't stand to be apart from her, but she didn't believe him. Truth was, he didn't trust her.

The one time she tried going out without Danny, she ended up at the hospital. It was a nightmare: she was screaming, he was screaming; she was slapping him, he was punching her; she was grabbing her purse off the dresser, he was holding her hand flat on the dresser, butting his cigarette out on the back of her hand. It ended with her in tears, him claiming it was an accident and a long wait down at the accident and emergency unit.

Michelle rubs the white scar on the back of her hand.

Danny said he loved Michelle, but she wasn't so sure. If this is love, she asked herself, why can it only be expressed in rage? Like the last time they went to the nightclub. Everyone was there—Kelly, Josephine, Cindy, even John Minardi, the assistant manager at Safeway. John was always cracking jokes about how the checkout chicks were his Charlie's Angels, only one better.

The girls were laughing, flashing their teeth at John in the fluorescent dark, especially Josephine. Once, when she was drunk, Josephine told Michelle that she wanted to marry John Minardi and have his babies because 'He's Cathlick an' I'm Cathlick—we're the only Cathlicks at Safeway, so we're meant f'each other.'

The Safeway gang were all up on the floor, dancing in a haphazard circle to Right Said Fred's "I'm Too Sexy" while Danny stood on the sidelines nursing a beer. With his black hair slicked back and his fluorescent white shirt, John looked good on the dance floor. He knew how to move. Kelly, Josephine, Cindy, and Michelle took turns to bump bums with him as they sang along. When Michelle's turn came, John moved behind her, put his hands on her hips and grooved his pelvis in time with hers—backwards and forwards, forwards and backwards. Josephine pulled a face, but Kelly and Cindy started squealing and clapping.

Then it happened.

Somebody with a leather jacket knocked Michelle aside.

John was on the floor—hair askew, blood splattered over his fluorescent shirt.

Danny was standing over him; collaring John with one hand, punching him in the head with the other.

Michelle saw Danny put his shoulder into each punch, saw the furious look in his face. Josephine jumped on Danny's back, but he flipped her off. John found his feet and swung wildly, but Danny ducked neatly, grabbed a fistful of John's coiffure, and kneed him in the face.

The commotion continued until one bouncer pinned Danny from behind and another marched up and kicked him hard in the balls.

Michelle tried to stop the bouncers, tried to explain it was all her fault, but they pushed her aside, took Danny down to the car park and kicked the animal out of him.

There are no headlights visible in the side mirror. The wind lashing through the open window blows away the edge of the air-freshener, unmasking the piss stink. Michelle doesn't know which is worse—leaving the window down and putting up with the smell or winding it up and being asphyxiated by the air-freshener.

Eight

Toby follows the beeping of the mobile, finds Suzie, still sitting cross-legged in her vacant parking bay, working her way up her forearm with the razor, carving Xs into her skin. She is humming as she works, arm weeping with blood.

'Hi,' he says.

'Hi y'self,' Suzie replies without looking up.

'What're you doin'?'

'Helping Sal with his spelling.'

'Sal?'

Suzie points over to Sal, who is spray painting the roof of a Commodore.

Toby scratches his head: 'What's he doin'?'

Suzie licks her razor clean, wraps it in her tissue, slides herself onto the bonnet of a Camry, says, 'Sal wants people on the moon to see his words.'

'What's he doin'?'

'Jeez. What'm I doin'? What's he doin'? What th'fuck're you doin'?

'What?'

'What? I just got the sack, that's what. Ronald fucken McDonald sacked me.'

'Why?'

'Why? Cos you pissed in Brendan's car, that's why.'

'Oh.'

'Right. You go an' piss in Brendan's car an' I laugh so he sacks me. Then he goes, *I know you've been handing out free Big Macs, too, cos I've kept a bun tally*. An' then he goes, *Your services are no longer required.*'

'A bun tally?'

Suzie nods, 'A fucken bun tally. Thanks a lot, arse-hole.'

'Look, Suzie, I'm sorry, orright. I just wanted to show you I'm not so gutless.'

'Great. Wonderful. You're not gutless.'

'What's the matter, but?'

'A hundred bucks is the matter.'

'A hundred bucks?'

'You heard.'

Perched on the Camry like a giant hood ornament, Suzie unwraps her tissue, resumes working on her arm. Toby leans against the side of the sedan. He is within arm's reach of Suzie. He wants to tell her about the baby he found alone in the house, but that seems meaningless right now.

'So,' he finally asks, 'What's your dad want?'

'A piece of me.'

'What're you goin' on about?'

She sighs: 'I was meant to get paid tonight.'

'But you didn't.'

'No. I got sacked—remember? An' now I've gotta go home and pay a fortnight's rent and board which is—guess how much?'

'A hundred dollars?'

'—bingo. An' I don't have it. I'm rooted.'

'What'll happen?'

'They'll both go off their faces. Dad can be fucken scary.'

'Really?'

'Yeah, really.'

'So what're y'gunna do?'

She shrugs her shoulders: 'You tell me.'

Nine

Brendan wants to carry Michelle over the threshold.

'Get real,' she says and carts her own suitcase through the door.

The lounge is small, but new: new coat of paint, new pine furniture, new TV.

'Home,' Brendan says.

'Nice,' Michelle replies with no real enthusiasm.

Brendan takes Michelle's suitcase to the bedroom and tosses it onto the unmade futon: 'Ignore the mess.'

'No worries.'

A portable TV sits on a chair at the foot of the bed. The room is cluttered with damp towels and discarded clothes.

'It needs a clean,' Brendan says—closing the door. He leads Michelle out to the kitchen. She follows, still carrying her wet floral dress in a plastic shopping bag.

Brendan points out all the major features: 'Microwave, fridge, dishwasher—everything you need. And they're all European appliances.'

'European,' Michelle repeats as though in a trance.

Another portable sits, Buddha-like, on the bare bench.

'Does the oven work?' Michelle asks.

Brendan glances at his watch: 'Um, dunno. Haven't used it yet.'

'You got a laundry?'

He thumbs in the direction of a door: 'Through there.'

Michelle checks, comes back without the plastic shopping bag and leans against the sink.

Brendan claps his hands together: 'So—do you like it?'

Michelle nods, says 'Nice' again.

'Great. Tremendous. It's a year old. This townhouse was the last of the four to sell so I got it for an excellent price, cos they were keen to off-load it. It's an investment property, really.'

Michelle stifles a yawn.

Brendan drones on: 'Course, it's really meant for a single person, but we'll manage. It'll be a squeeze though...anyway'—he pads off into the bedroom, still talking loudly; Michelle trails into the lounge, sinks into the couch—'you haven't got much stuff an' we'll be able t'do stuff together. Y'know, go to the gym and the beach and even water-skiing, once I buy my speedboat and you lose some weight.'

'Yeah?'

'I'll sign you up for aerobics tonight, okay? So you can start tomorrow after work.'

Brendan comes out to the lounge, his sugar-bun soft thighs squeezed into bicycle shorts, wearing a sloppy T-shirt to hide his Big Mac belly, kisses Michelle on the mouth: 'I'll have you shipshape in no time... Looking forward to tomorrow?'

'Guess so.'

'Good. I'm off—back soon.'

They kiss again, then Brendan bolts, calling out, 'Seeya.' The door slams behind him.

Michelle waits until Brendan's car drives off before she starts inspecting the unit at her own leisure: opening cupboards, wardrobes and drawers, picking through Brendan's CD and video collection, checking the contents of the fridge. There are no books in the unit, just a slagheap of magazines: magazines about speedboats, magazines about sport, magazines about bodybuilding, magazines about small businesses, magazines about naked women. Michelle sorts idly through the pile, leafs through a girlie magazine, then returns to the fridge—pulling out a beer and a packet of chocolate biscuits—flops back on the couch, fiddles with the remote until the TV clicks on, starts surfing through the channels, looking for something to watch.

Ten

'Do you have a smoke?'

'Nup.'

'I'd kill for a smoke.'

'I'm broke.'

Suzie tisks: '*You're* broke.'

Toby kicks some loose stones. They skitter across the bitumen, ricochet against the door of an AU Falcon.

'I should go home.'

'Don't.'

'M'dad keeps sendin' threatenin' SMSs.'

'Prick. You should stay with me.'

'Yeah, right.'

Suzie cracks her knuckles: 'Fuck. I wanna get away.'

'Where?'

'Anywhere. Anywhere that's not here.'

'Like Disneyland?'

She smiles: 'Yeah.'

'D'you know where I wanna go?'

Before Suzie can reply, they are interrupted.

'HEY! HEY YOU!'

A red-faced man with a huge moustache is charging towards Suzie and Toby, yelling. Three young children, a boy and two girls, trail behind the Red-Faced Man, who is the same height as Toby, but much older and heavier: equipped with a hefty beer gut, bull neck, and meaty forearms.

'What?' Suzie asks.

Instead of replying, the Red-Faced Man pulls Suzie by the arms, dragging her off the Camry.

'Piss off,' Suzie says.

Then the Red-Faced Man starts shoving Toby—sending him

backward across the parking bay.

'YOU DID IT—DIDN'T YOU?!' he screams at Toby.

'Dad?' The boy, who is aged around eight, has stopped eating his cheeseburger, and is standing apart from his two younger sisters, who are sucking fretfully on their Cokes.

'Not now Craig!' the Red-Faced Man orders.

Toby tries fending the man off, but is shoved harder.

'What's your fucken problem?' Toby asks.

The Red-Faced Man pokes Toby in the chest with a meaty finger: 'SMART-ARSE! DON'T PULL MY CHAIN! I KNOW LITTLE SHITS LIKE YOU!'

'Dad?' Craig's forehead is crinkled.

'Leave him alone!' Suzie yells.

She jumps onto the Red-Faced Man's back, but he throws her—slapping her flat on her back against the bitumen.

'STAY OUTTA THIS! This is between him an' me!' the Red-Faced Man bawls at Suzie. He backs Toby against an old Cortina, fastens a hand around his throat.

'Dad? Dad?!' Craig pleads, fit to burst into tears.

'CRAIG! NOT NOW!'

Wheezing for breath, Suzie picks herself up, yells 'Leave him alone!' and runs at the Red-Faced Man—rabbit-punching him in the back of the head.

'FUCK!' howls the Red-Faced Man.

Stung, he backhands Suzie across the cheek, sits her on her arse. Still in a chokehold, Toby watches the Red-Faced Man's face deepen, turn crimson. He starts cuffing Toby about the head, goading him.

'Can't you keep her on a leash?' he asks Toby with a sneer.

Toby just stares.

Suzie gets up, slaps at the Red-Faced Man again and is dumped on the ground again.

'Can't you make her heel?' the Red-Faced Man gives Toby a churlish smile—his voice jocular, menacing. 'What's your name, sonny?'

'Daniel,' Toby says.

'Hullo Daniel. I'm Steve Finch. You vandalized my wife's car, Daniel.'

With that, Finch punches Toby in the solar plexus, making him jump from the force of his blow.

'Toby!' Suzie yells.

'Toby?' Finch stops, leans over Toby, who is writhing on the hot bitumen. 'Is that your real name, Daniel? Toby?'

Suzie jumps on Finch's back—scratching at him, pulling his hair.

'DAD!' Craig cries—bawling now.

'Fuck!' Finch snaps his elbow back hard into Suzie's face, hitting her just above the right eye.

'Jeez,' Finch says—two-long scratch marks arc from the corners of his mouth to the flaps of his earlobes.

Suzie crumples to her hands and knees, blood seeping from a gash above her eyebrow, making fresh stains on the oil-splattered parking bay.

Dabbing at his watermelon smile, Finch crouches over Suzie.

'Sorry 'bout that,' he says, 'But you shouldn't try eye-gouging a bloke, now, shouldya?'

'Dad?'

Finch's voice softens, sounds paternal: 'Craig. Stop bawling an' go back to the car. Take your sisters.'

He turns to Suzie: 'You orright? I hate hitting women usually.'

'Get fucked,' Suzie spits.

'Fine, then. If that's the way you want it, y'slag.'

Finch goes over to Toby, rests his boot on Toby's chest: 'Toby who? What's your last name, sonny, and don't give me any Daniel bullshit.'

'Purcell,' Toby moans.

'An' where d'you live Toby Purcell? Huh?'

'Another Avenue.'

'You better sonny. You better. See you later.'

Finch walks across the car park, back to his car and his children.

Eleven

Brendan sleeps as he lives: hogging the side of the futon closest to the bathroom door, not bothering to dream. Michelle listens to him suck in oxygen, blow out carbon dioxide; wishes she could smother him with her pillow, cut off his dick and shove it up his fat arse.

In the kitchen, the refrigerator hums to life. Michelle listens to its motor chug away as she lies in her sweat. Beads of perspiration dampen her hair, congregate in the hollow between her breasts.

Michelle wants to take a shower and scrub until her skin peels off. She wants to scream but is afraid she wouldn't be able to scream loudly enough to be truly heard.

Big mistake. She makes a big mistake. She says, 'I love you.'

Brendan comes home from the gym and Michelle starts kissing him. She's in a hurry—as if she wants to get it out of the way, as if she's trying to prove something to herself. They tumble into the bedroom, onto the futon, strip each other. Brendan is on top of Michelle, grunting. She can smell his sweat. He is excited, Brendan is; making the futon creak. Michelle kisses his mouth, looks into his eyes, then says it.

'I love you.'

And everything grinds to a halt. Panting, sweating, his pathetic dick still inside her, Brendan stops. He looks disgusted.

'What'd you fucken say that for?'

Michelle opens her mouth to speak but nothing comes out.

'Don't be stupid,' Brendan says.

Then he resumes fucking her. And, as he fucks her, Michelle lies still as a stone, feels him pound against her, hammer her out of shape. By the time he has finished, Michelle is deep within herself.

She lies there, perfectly still. She is trying to grow accustomed to her surroundings.

Twelve

The futon is hard, the unit brand new—not crowded with history like Mum's place. Michelle shifts, causing the futon's pine base to creak. Brendan stirs, mutters a few incongruous words, rolls over. The futon creaks some more.

Brendan does not sleep like Danny. Danny kicked and swore and sweated and snorted like a bull—thrashing about in the dark at whatever it was that visited him in his dreams. Sometimes he named names.

'...Toby!...Toby!...Toby!...'

One night he kicked Michelle awake, screaming out Toby's name in his sleep with a voice that, for once, was more fearful than furious. Michelle leapt out of bed, stood against the wall, watched Danny fight in the darkness.

For Danny, there is no rest.

It took a while to find Danny after the nightclub bouncers had finished with him. He was under a Subaru in the car park, shaking from shock. Michelle grabbed one of his motorcycle boots, and, using her little black dress as a counterweight, slipped and shimmied and dragged him out into the open, lay her tizzed head upon his ragged chest to ensure he was still breathing. His eyes opened.

'What didja fucken do that for?' Michelle bawled.

Shaking, cradling his broken ribs with his left arm, Danny hauled himself upright, locked his right arm straight to brace the weight of his upper torso: 'Where have the cunts gone?'

'Who?'

'The fucken bouncers.'

'Back inside.'

'But I haven't finished with 'em.'

It took awhile, but Danny got to his feet, staggered around the car park screaming: 'COME BACK! FIGHT ME YOU GUTLESS MONGRELS!' And, when he couldn't find anyone to fight, Danny went mad. There was no other word for what Michelle witnessed. He flailed about with insane rage—shattering passenger windows with his fists, kicking off side mirrors, smashing headlights, snapping aerials, wrenching the bumper off an old XB Falcon and using it to cave in a Monaro's windscreen and club its canary-yellow duco. Finally, broken, out of breath and bloodied, he sank to the ground and cried. Cried in great looping sobs. Cried as though there was no end to the grief.

Lying in the dark, Michelle wishes she could cry like that.

Ghosts

One

My hands are so small they are as translucent as jelly fish limbs. I form one of my jelly fish hands into a fist and shove it into my mouth for safekeeping. I am anxious. When I close my eyes I can see the shadows outside the Purcell's house, lapping against the brick walls, rubbing against the windows, waiting for the lights to go out so they can slip beneath the doors, come inside.

One shadow circles the house silently—the shadow of a man moving through the darkness—the ghost of a long dead night. It searches now like its concrete self once did—waiting for the lights to go out—waiting for an opening.

Just as it did so long ago.

The shadow is moving slowly—careful to keep the metal of its rifle and jerry can from kissing.

Two

Mum reads to Gran from *TV Week* until the older woman drifts into infant sleep, her dreams dancing off into the darkness.

'...Kinky Kylie says her heart was broken by the raunchy romance. *Michael was my great love, the man who turned me from a little girl into a real woman, but now he's gone. And I'm heartbroken,* she told a friend recently... Gran? You awake Gran?...The End,' Mum says and rolls the magazine into a baton.

Closing, then snibbing Gran's door behind her, Mum walks out to the lounge. She tries turning on the TV once again. Still busted.

'Dead,' she tells the empty room.

Deciding to make herself a cup of tea before heading off for work, Mum plugs in the electric jug—stands at the sink waiting for the water to boil. Framed by darkness, Mum's reflection stares in at her from the window.

I see the shadow outside—prowling—moving across the loose gravel drive without making a sound. No longer alive—no longer dead—it glides into the backyard.

Sees Jacki through the window. Turns to steam.

Mum's reflection looks more like a skull than her own countenance. She touches her face. Yes, it is still warm. Still alive. But for how much longer? When she dies will the ghost of her face remain in the kitchen window?

It's like Hiroshima, she thinks.

Once, Mum watched a documentary on the telly about the atomic bomb. Now, her mind is flooded with the furry pictures beamed through her busted TV—footage of the mushroom cloud, the molten aftermath, civilian faces radiated to the consistency of burnt toast, the shadow of a man vaporized into a flight of concrete stairs he was ascending the instant the shockwave hit. How did that feel? One instant walking up the stairs, perhaps taking them two at a time, then a giant flashlight triggers, followed by the sound wave—a thunderclap—and that man was no longer flesh and bone, but a shadow burnt into concrete steps.

Mum feels herself vaporizing. Each morning, she gets up, brushes her teeth and inspects herself; checking to ensure she's still all there. Has another piece of young Jacki disappeared? Which part? Mum's death, her vanishing, is in time lapse—too slow to catch with the naked eye. She hadn't noticed her hair fading until, one morning, she awoke to find she was no longer brunette, but salt-and-pepper—a steel-wool grey—one day closer to becoming a shadow on concrete stairs.

Something Gran said when Mum was helping her brush her teeth has set her thinking. Gran is standing in front of the mirror, brushing the remnants of her teeth, while Mum guides her hand.

Gran catches her own eye in the mirror. Stops brushing.

'Who's that?' she sprays toothpaste froth over the mirror.

'That's you,' Mum replies, 'That's Gran.'

Gran mulls over that fact, slops the toothpaste around in her mouth, looks at her daughter: 'You're Jacki?'

'I'm Jacki,' Mum nods.

This agitates Gran: 'I'm a dancer, but. How'd I get like this? I'm a dancer, but. I am.'

'Yes you are,' Mum soothes.

'I am?'

'A beautiful dancer,' Mum says.

Gran goes to bed happy because she's been reassured she's a beautiful dancer, but Mum's unsettled. She can't help thinking: One minute I'm Jacki, next minute I'm Mum. One minute I'm a person, next minute I'm a shadow. One minute I'm young, next minute I'm bone old and not yet forty.

There's no stopping life, Mum decides. No turning back the mistakes. No starting over. You just live with your mistakes. Carry them. Pay for them.

Three

The whistle squeals.

Steam cascades from the kettle, frosts the window, clouds the ceiling. Mum is motionless, anchored to the sink, staring at the ghost of her reflection.

Mum cannot remember when or how Jacki met Gary. She just remembers that Jacki was young: too young and too bloody stupid.

It was back when the Purcells lived down the peninsula in a two-bedroom fibro shack—Gran and Pa in one bedroom, Jacki the other. Most nights Jacki lay in bed, listening to them brawl. Pa would come home from the pub and toss Gran around; bouncing her off the walls, throwing drunken, round-arm punches that Gran either ducked, fended off, or wore. By the time she was fifteen Mum was climbing out the window every night to escape; floating up and down the streets, eating fish-and-chips on the footpath, feet in the gutter, bluffing her way into the Cricketer's Arms—where men with boozy breath pinched her arse with nicotine-stained fingers, invited her out the back, shouted her a pot and a bag of chips. She was doing anything to keep out from under the asbestos roof of that two bedroom shack. It was around this time, somewhere between the fish'n'chip shop and the Cricketer's Arms, that Jacki met Gary Nagle.

Gary was older, in his mid-twenties. He owned a new car, was paying off his own house and making a packet as a plumber. Jacki liked Gary Nagle—liked the way he bought her presents and bought her beers, liked the way he kept her out of Pa's way, liked the way he was grown-up, liked the way he made her feel grown-up too, liked the way he drove her around in his new car, liked the way that new car smelled, liked the way he called her Little Jacki.

When Jacki found out she was pregnant she told herself she should be happy because she had something inside her that was all hers—something no one could take. Something special.

Living with Gary was all right, too, so long as Jacki stayed within the perimeters, did exactly as she was told. Jacki had four main duties: fucking, feeding, cooking, and cleaning. Waiting for her lord and master to return, Jacki sat out on the back step sometimes, smoking as Danny played bare-arsed in the dirt lawn and Ringo the collie ran in circles—straining against the chain Gary had pegged into the ground.

Jacki tried not to hate Gary—tried settling for the pragmatic approach. She depended on Gary. He put money on the table, kept her and Danny off the streets. Without him she was a drop-out with a baby, no friends, no trade, no money, no support, and no options.

Gary gave Jacki a list of tasks to perform when he left for work—anything from mowing the lawn and mopping the floor to cleaning out the garage—then he came home late, stinking of beer and cigarettes, and inspected her work. If Gary judged Jacki's work to be up to scratch, she was rewarded, receiving a five dollar bonus in her weekly housekeeping allowance. 'Go an' treat y'self,' Gary would say indulgently. If she didn't pass muster, Jacki was punished—losing her cigarette or television privileges.

The front door closes. Footsteps travel through the lounge to the kitchen, come to a halt behind Jacki.

'Mum?'

Toby clicks off the squealing kettle.

'Mum?' he repeats—his voice urgent.

Toby's voice rouses Jacki from her reverie. But the closer she comes to answering her son, the further from her shadow years Jacki moves. By the time she responds, Jacki will be Mum once more.

Mum keeps staring at herself in the window.

'You killed the telly,' she says.

'I know.'

'I can't afford another one. What's Gran gunna watch now?'

'I'm sorry, Mum, but you gotta take Suzie to the doctor.'

Mum pours boiled water into her mug, jiggles a tea bag: 'Suzie Who?'

Suzie pipes up: 'Suzie Collier. I'm Toby's girlfriend.'

Mum turns away from her reflection and takes a long, hard look at a small pale girl with blood caked over her face, hands, neck, and uniform.

'Hullo,' Suzie says, offering a bloodied hand.

Mum shakes the hand, turns to Toby: 'What did you friggin' do to her?'

'Me? I didn't do anything. Some bloke beat us both up outside Maccas.'

'What'd you do?'

'Nuthin'.'

'You been stealing stuff?'

'No.'

Mum slaps Toby: 'Don't lie!'

'Let's go,' Suzie tugs at Toby's sleeve.

'No,' Mum tells Suzie. 'Come here. Into the light.'

Suzie obeys.

Mum turns to Toby: 'Get one of the old towels from the wardrobe.'

Once Toby has gone, she asks Suzie again whether he hurt her.

'No,' Suzie says.

'You can tell me.'

'It wasn't Toby. Some guy punched Toby and thumped me.'

'Good,' Mum nods. 'This needs stitches. I'll drive you down to the clinic. Get Toby and meet me outside.'

Mum takes her mug of tea out to the car, starts the motor and sits there idling, sipping the sweet black brew.

Suzie comes out first, holding a fluffy pink towel to her head.

'That's a good towel,' Mum yells out the window.

'Sorry. I'll get another one,' Suzie says.

'Too late now. Get in the front.'

Suzie slams the door and the two women sit in silence. Mum gently revs the engine to keep it from stalling.

'So—Suzie, is it?' Mum asks.

'Yep.'

'Didn't know Toby had a girlfriend.'

'Oh, well.'

'How old're you?'

Suzie licks her lips, which are dry and taste like salt: 'Sixteen.'

'Y'like Toby?'

'Yep.'

Mum shakes her head slowly. The windscreen is covered in dust and crusted bird shit, cracked down the driver's side. Mum squirts water and flicks on the wipers, smearing an even film of grime over the windscreen. Mum tisks, flicks off the wipers.

'Where's Toby?'

'In the dunny.'

Mum sips her tea, squeezes the accelerator.

'How's y'head? Orright?'

'Yep.'

Beepbeep! Beepbeep! Suzie doesn't bother to read the SMS message.

'Who's that?'

'Prob'ly my Dad.'

'D'you wanna use the phone?'

Suzie shakes her head: 'I don't wanna talk to him...I'm going to go an' live with my mum in New York.'

'New York?'

'Yep. My mum's a model, you know. She's on the covers of magazines and stuff over there.'

'Nice.'

'Yep. I want Toby to come an' visit.'

'I'm sure he'll want to visit.'

'Here he is.'

Toby runs across the drive wearing Danny's leather jacket over Danny's overalls.

'About bloody time!' Mum scowls as she slots the car into reverse.

Four

Shadows and heat blend and cook—forming a many-coloured fog. Heavy and humid, the fog crawls across the carpet, slides under doors, seeps into undeveloped dreams, sets off photochemical reactions.

Short of breath, drowning in the humidity, Gran wakes.

She knows she is dying.

I've had it, she thinks.

Gran's spirit sits lightly in her chest.

She thinks, Life is like a big biscuit factory. I'm at the end of the line, but there's another batch gettin' cooked up orready.

Knowing this, Gran feels no gladness, no grief—just the immensity of the inevitable.

Five

Mum steers up the freeway off-ramp—slows to sixty, stops at the traffic lights with the engine turning over.

'You busted the TV, y'know,' Mum says over her shoulder.

Toby shifts in his seat: 'I know. You told me orready.'

'It's wrecked, y'know. Useless.'

'Sorry.'

'Gran watches the telly all the time. What's she gunna do now, hey? Didja ever think of that? Course not—bust every friggin' thing I own.'

'I said I was sorry. Fuck.'

Mum guns the accelerator as the lights flash green; Toby stares out the window, Suzie pries the towel away from her head.

'How're you going, Suzie?' Mum asks.

'Fine, thanks.'

'Nearly there.'

The Kingswood drones along until it reaches an intersection with a service station on one corner and a medical clinic on the other—pulls into the clinic's car park. Mum parks directly outside the clinic, which resembles a converted 7/11 store. They all climb out.

'Don't worry about locking the door,' Mum tells Suzie. 'If someone wants this heap of shit, good luck to 'em.'

A man wearing a white dustcoat is standing behind the front counter, reading a book; a sign on the wall behind him reads 24 HOUR CARE in big gold lettering. Mum leads the way up to the counter, stands there, waiting to catch the man's eye. Suzie stands behind her. Toby scouts around: every spare seat in the waiting room is taken—sickly children are curled up on their parents' laps, watching *Thelma and Louise* on a TV screwed into the ceiling at the corner of the room. Toby parks himself under the TV, arms folded, head craned.

'Are you the doctor?' Mum asks the man in the white dust-coat that is old and badly stained around the sleeves.

The man doesn't look up from his book, a sloppy translation of *War and Peace* that he's been struggling to read all summer.

'No,' he replies, annoyed. 'I'm the nurse.'

Suzie pipes up: 'I wanna see the doctor.'

'Join the crowd. Have you been here before?'

As he talks to Suzie in a thoroughly bored tone, keeping his place in *War and Peace* with a thermometer, the nurse pulls out a pen and rummages through the disarray of the counter for the Medicare card register: '...Now—where's that register gone?... Right...Okay. Been here before?'

'Yes.'

'Name?'

'Suzie Collier.'

The nurse punches Suzie's name into the computer, taps his pen impatiently on the desktop.

'Here we are—Suzanne. You live in Another?'

Suzie nods.

Noticing her uniform, he smiles sarcastically: 'So, what happened to you? Ask the wrong person if they wanted a sundae?'

Suzie scowls: 'I fell over.'

'Show me.'

Suzie removes the towel, knotted with her blood, and the nurse leans across the counter, pronounces an instant diagnosis: 'Three or four stitches. You'll live...The wait's at least an hour.'

'An hour?' Mum splutters. 'I gotta get to work.'

The nurse, assuming Mum is Suzie's mum, sneers: 'Well, Mrs Collier, if that bothers you, you can drive half an hour down the road and wait two to three hours at the General's accident and emergency.'

'I'll wait,' Suzie says.

'Grab a seat,' the nurse says and immerses himself in *War and Peace* again.

Toby wanders over from the TV, is told about the backlog of patients.

'I can't stay, Toby. I've gotta work,' Mum says.

'Yeah. An' Suzie's gotta see the doctor,' he retorts.

'I need the money.'

'I'll be right,' Suzie says. 'I'll call my dad.'

Toby jumps in: 'No you fucken won't.'

'Her parents should know,' Mum says.

'S'cuse me,' the nurse butts in, 'I'm trying to read here.'

The three of them drift towards the door.

'Orright,' Toby says to Mum, 'You go an' we'll stay. We can find our own way back.'

Mum glances at her watch: 'You sure?'

'Yeah.'

Suzie nods in accord.

Relieved, Mum smiles: 'Good. I gotta go. Nice t'meet you, Suzie.'

Mum hurries out the door.

Suzie and Toby sit on the carpet. She leans against the wall; he leans against her—resting his head on her shoulder. A black leather arm falls across Suzie's lap. She plays with the arm, liking the feel of the leather.

'I'd kill for a smoke,' she whispers.

Toby does not answer. He is already asleep.

Six

Thelma and Louise drive off the edge of the cliff—victorious—launching their convertible into the sky. The screen freezes: credits roll.

'Good ending,' Suzie says to nobody in particular.

She chews her nails, desperate for a cigarette.

Across from Suzie, a young woman cradles a baby. The baby starts to cry. Suzie watches the woman unbutton her blouse, unclip her bra, and nestle the baby's mouth against the warmth of her breast with practised ease. The crying is replaced by a contented suckling sound.

With her free hand the woman cradles the back of her baby's head. Catching Suzie's eye, she gives a tired smile. Suzie looks away.

Seven

Life's orbit is laborious, but undeniable—the turning of a mountainous tide. Birth and death lap every shoreline, drag away even the strongest swimmer.

Gran floats in the shallows, waiting for the tide to take her, bobbing between birth and death with each heartbeat.

Tonight, the death tide is strong. Gran feels it drag against her chest, feels her spirit rise into her mouth, float on her tongue, daring to be spoken. Gran wants to pray, yet doesn't know what to ask for. Beg forgiveness? No, she thinks, There is so much—too much—to forgive.

Gran can feel and see the shadows in her room. Some are colours and shapes, others the ghosts of animals and people—they seduce her with their caresses.

Gran sees the ghost with the gun and jerry can. It lingers for a few minutes, then floats away.

Another shadow levitates above the bed.

Jack, Gran thinks. She reaches for the apparition: a dark little man with slicked back hair smiling down at her. 'Jack,' she croons. Gran closes her eyes and is dancing again, wheeling across the polished floorboards. When she opens her eyes, though, Jack is gone...*Doug*, Gran sucks heavy air into her addled lungs...and, in his place, is Pa—a death mask looming down at Gran from the ceiling. Pleading, accusing.

Pa died just as he lived. Pissed as a fart, he staggered through the front door one night, knocked one of Gran's hand-painted plates off the wall and started bellowing.

'Woman! Woman!'

He thundered down the hall, hunting for Gran as he unfastened his belt, threading it around the horny knuckles of his right hand.

'Woman!'

Gran was in the lounge, watching telly.

When Pa reached the doorway he lifted his fist: 'There y'are.'

Gran leapt to her feet, but her husband's frame filled the doorway, there was no escape.

'So where'd y'get the bright bloody idea, eh?'

'Pa?'

'Pa Pa Pa Pa!' he mimicked, took a run-up, sank his boot into the crystal cabinet, pulled out Gran's best china, spread it across the carpet, danced it to pieces under his boots, his face bright red, his unfastened trousers falling down around his hairy arse.

'Zorba!' he wheezed—hitching up his pants.

'My china!'

Pa narrowly missed Gran with a teacup.

'Put plates on the walls so a fella breaks them, willya?'

He swiped at Gran with his belted paw, but she ducked, moved into the vacant doorway. Pa made a lunge for Gran but stopped abruptly... let his pants fall down...grimaced in pained surprise, then fright...sagged to his knees as though about to pray over the busted china. Gran backed away as Pa sank to the carpet. Convulsed. Turned purple. Shat himself. Clutched at the air. Pa's eyes were in Gran's; burning, not blinking, pleading. Gran left the room, but came back with a kitchen chair and a packet of cigarettes. She set the chair in the doorway, just out of Pa's reach, and lit herself a fag.

She sat there, smoking, until the fire in Pa's eyes burnt out.

Eight

A young woman dressed neatly in jeans and a white polo shirt comes out from the surgery, stands beside the grumpy nurse, calls out, 'Suzanne Collier?'

Suzie leaves Toby sleeping, and, still pressing Mum's towel to her head, follows the woman into a sparsely furnished room that smells of antiseptic. Inside, Suzie sits in one of the two metal chairs, scans about for a third person, a doctor, but the only other person in the room is the young woman, who's now perched on the corner of the desk, hands clasped.

'Hello. I'm Doctor Shu,' the young woman says.

She is smaller than Suzie, Dr Shu, with short black hair and a square Chinese face.

'You're the doctor?'

Dr Shu smiles, picks up Suzie's patient card, keeps talking as she reads: 'How did you hurt your head, Suzanne?'

Suzie slumps in her chair: 'Do you have a smoke? I'd kill for a smoke.'

Dr Shu points to a No Smoking sign: 'Sorry.'

'I could smoke outside.'

'Let's talk about your head.'

'Someone beat me and Toby up.'

'Do you know this someone?'

'No. He just came up to us in the car park, yelling at us, an' then started beating us up.'

'And who is Toby?'

'Toby's my boyfriend.'

'How is he?'

'He's orright.'

'Where was he struck?'

'Um...the guy punched him in the guts.'

'Did this man hurt your arm, too?'

Suzie's surprised: 'My arm?'

'Yes, you've got some nasty lacerations.'

Suzie had cut away the memory of her weeping arm.

'Oh,' she says. 'That. It's nuthin.'

'Let me be the judge of that. Now, let's take a look at your head.'

Reluctantly, Suzie takes the towel from her forehead, prying the fabric from the wound. Dr Shu fetches a plastic dish, tears open a swab and starts dabbing at Suzie's forehead, making it tingle, sting.

'Don't worry, it looks much worse than it is,' Dr Shu says. 'But I'll have to give you an injection before I stitch you up so the stitches won't hurt. Okay?'

Dr Shu makes Suzie lie down on the examination table, pulls a lamp over and sets to work cleaning the wound, gives Suzie an injection that makes her swear. At first, the injection is excruciating, a liquid metal in Suzie's head, then it soothes. Suzie feels detached, impervious, a step removed, only vaguely aware that something is probing her outer casing—just like she does when she cuts herself.

Suzie stares straight up into the lamp. Black spots pulsate before her eyes.

Dr Shu's voice is distant, asking Suzie questions about McDonald's and her arm. Suzie answers each question in a dreamy tone.

'Have you been feeling down lately?'

Suzie's voice swims back up to Dr Shu, '...falling down?'

'No. Feeling down. Depressed.'

'...fallingdowndepressed?'

Dr Shu threads the needle through a flap of Suzie's skin, the sensation tickles.

Suzie giggles, 'I need a smoke.'

'Uh-huh. How did these cuts get in your arm?'

'Oh, they just got there.'

'Have you been in a car accident?'

Suzie laughs, 'A car accident? I can't drive.'

Dr Shu finishes the stitching in silence, sits Suzie up while she dresses the wound. Dizzy from the anaesthetic, Suzie blinks repeatedly as she tries to force her world back in focus.

'You all right?' Dr Shu asks.

'Yeah. The light was in my eyes, but.'

Dr Shu massages Suzie's stitched head, then pulls out a cotton swab and sticking plaster—gives Suzie a third eyebrow.

'There,' Dr Shu sighs. 'Now lets look at your arm.'

'It's orright.'

'Let me be the judge of that.'

'An'...ah...I wanna ask about something else.'

'In a minute.'

Dr Shu's forehead furrows with three vertical lines, just between her eyebrows, as she cleans Suzie's arm. The doctor walks back to the desk and scrawls notes on Suzie's patient card. Suzie turns to try to see what she is writing, but the desk is too far from the bench.

Suzie notices something odd: a pre-pubescent girl with a cute-as-a-button blonde bob is sitting on the other corner of the desk, kicking her legs in the air because they cannot reach the floor, smiling knowingly. The girl is very pretty, with slender limbs, blue eyes, and honey-brown skin. She's wearing an oversized T-shirt with Reebok printed on the front in red, along with light grey bicycle shorts, Reebok cross-trainers, and white Reebok socks. The only blemish to the girl's ensemble is a ribbon of blood that flows from her left cheek to her throat, staining her Reebok T-shirt.

Suzie had forgotten how much she hated Annette Norman.

Dobber cunt, she thinks.

Annette Norman mouths *I hate you.*

Dr Shu is still scribbling away, making secret computations.

'You're a bloodsucker,' Annette declares.

'Fuck off,' Suzie hisses.

Dr Shu stops writing. 'What was that?'

Annette smiles winningly.

'Nuthin',' Suzie says.

Dr Shu tucks some hair back behind her ear, keeps writing as she talks, 'So what was it you wanted to talk about, Suzanne?'

'Huh?'

'You said you wanted to ask me about something.'

'Yeah,' Suzie clears her throat. 'Um...do you do other stuff?'

'What other stuff did you have in mind?'

'Abortions.'

Dr Shu drops her pen; gives Suzie her full attention.

'Why? Are you pregnant, Suzanne?'

'Me? Nup...don't think so.'

'Well—are you sexually active?'

'Yep.'

'Do you use contraceptives?'

'Nup.'

'Have you missed a period?'

Suzie folds her arms. Her head feels woozy and she can hear Annette Norman giggling.

'I won't tell your mother,' Dr Shu says.

'No, you won't,' Suzie shoots back.

'We can give you a pregnancy test.'

'It's orright. I'm not pregnant. I'm just wondering, that's all—if I need to, y' know, I wanna know where to go, what to do.'

Dr Shu looks dubious. She touches Suzie's lacerated arm: 'And how did this happen?'

'What?'

'Did you do this yourself?'

Annette sticks both hands in the air, squeals: 'She did! She did!'

Suzie shoots Annette a killing look.

'Suzanne?'

'Huh? Aw, no. I didn't do it. It must've happened when I fell over.'

'Liar! Liar! Pants on fire!' Annette yells.

Dr Shu starts cleaning Suzie's arm, applying antiseptic: 'Do your parents know you're here?'

'Yeah. My mum dropped me off,' Suzie lies.

'Is your mother here now? I'd like to talk to her.'

'You can't. She's gone to work,' Suzie lies, desperate to get back out into the night air. 'She's a model. Real busy. Toby an' me are catching a taxi home.'

'Where's your father?'

'He pissed off, didn't he? He used to bash us bad, but Mum stood up to him one day and he shot through. Haven't heard from him since, just the odd card. Yeah, she's gutsy, my Mum, she wouldn't leave me with that prick...but she's not out front. She's gone. If you don't believe me go and ask the guy out there. He saw Mum drop us off.'

'Wait here.'

Dr Shu closes the door behind her.

With the coast clear, Annette jumps off the desk—saunters over to Suzie.

'Blood sucker,' she catcalls.

'Dobber cunt,' Suzie hisses.

Annette's hand goes over her mouth: 'The C-word! I'm really gunna dob on you now.'

'That's all you do. Teacher's fucken pet.'

Annette gives a vexed hurrumph, then starts doing star jumps, counting 'one, two, three, four, five, six...'

Suzie rubs her head, watches Annette's performance.

'...seven, eight, nine...'

'What're you doing?'

'...getting ready for netball season...twelve, thirteen, fourteen...'

'No. What're y'doin' here?'

'Miss Munro...seventeen, eighteen, nineteen, twenty. There!'

Annette stops jumping up and down, puts her hands on her hips, puffs lightly: 'I've got to keep fit for netball. I'm wing attack—lots of running.'

'What the fuck're y'doin' here?'

'Cos Miss Munro asked me to. She said you needed guidance.'

'Fuck off.'

Annette's pretty face distorts: 'You fuck off! Bitch!'

Dr Shu opens the door—and Annette's snarl melts into her I'm-an-angel face.

'That guy toldja—didn't he?' Suzie demands.

Dr Shu nods: 'I just needed to check a few things. Now, I'll just finish patching up your arm. There's nothing serious there. It'll be fine so long as you keep the lacerations clean and don't allow any infections to develop. Your stitches will need to come out in seven days. When they come out they will leave a slight scar, but that will fade. Now, you can either call ahead and set an appointment or just drop by like you did tonight—whichever suits you...Now, Suzanne, I'm going to have to report this to the child protection services, you know. They may want to talk to you and your mother.'

'She swore at me, too,' Annette volunteers.

'I don't care,' Suzie says.

Dr Shu finishes dabbing antiseptic cream on Suzie's weeping arm.

Nine

Toby can't help himself. Just as I am always dreaming of Suzie he is always dreaming of Danny.

...Danny daring Toby to piss on the electric fence...Danny elbowing Lionel Blackmore in the face...Danny leering as he tells Toby 'I'm charged and ready to go'...Danny in his leathers, falling, suspended against a brilliant yellow canvas...

I see Danny, too.

Turning within Suzie's womb my mind yawns open—and past, present, and future rush in—so many broken pieces combining into a larger, more confusing puzzle piece. Depending on their angle, at different times, different images capture my attention—loom closer—sometimes startling me, sometimes making me kick.

At those moments I want to call to Danny—rouse him—chase his images from my head. Like now. I see a house burning in the night (a canvas of orange). I see a man running from the house, ablaze (a canvas of black). I see a boy lying face-down on a hospital bed (a canvas of red). I see a white fluorescent shirt splattered with blood (red again). I see a leather-clad figure catapulted through the air (a canvas of yellow).

The images shimmer with violence.

I kick, but I cannot escape the images. I see Danny as a boy hiding under the bed in Mum's room—fists clenched—watching his father's heavy work-boots lead his mother's thin bare ankles and feet in a brutal dance. The left boot steps forward and the bare feet stutter backwards, lose step altogether, fall over. Pregnant, bloodied, out of step, Mum never looks at Danny—never gives his hiding place away. Instead she looks up at her partner—begs Gary not to kick her in the stomach.

I kick again.

Ten

Toby is still hiding under the bed looking through Danny's eyes when Suzie shakes him awake—pulls him back into his own body, into the clinic's waiting room.

'Come on,' Suzie says.

She is tense around the mouth, has a white bandage stuck above her right eyebrow and yellow antiseptic smeared on her arm. She is even paler than normal.

'How'd it go?' Toby asks.

'Let's get the fuck outta here.'

'That good.'

Suzie's already at the door, impatient. Toby catches up, asks her whether she's all right.

'No, I'm not orright,' Suzie says and pushes through the swinging doors into the night air. Toby and Suzie orientate themselves, then trudge across the car park—a pretty little shadow of a girl wearing Reebok skips after them.

Eleven

Gran opens her eyes again. Thinks, *Jesus.*

Jack's hovering directly above her. So close she could reach into the hollow of his eyes with her fingers, run her open hand over his handsome face.

Eyes watery, Gran lies perfectly still—afraid to move, afraid to open her mouth to speak. Her soul is a lozenge on her tongue; sucked paper-thin, the edges sharp enough to cut the tissue of her mouth.

Jack's shadow smiles—the same winning smile he gave Gran down on the beach when he said 'no worries'. A black-and-white newsreel flickers in Gran's head of that time down at the beach. How they danced and danced.

Her head was so giddy.

They were spinning so fast.

She could barely keep pace.

Marvellous, Gran thinks.

It was bloody marvellous.

Jack was handsome and sure of himself. His breath smelt like peppermint. After they danced, he took Gran down to the beach where he kissed her and unbuttoned her and made promises he would never keep.

Gran is smiling.

No regrets now, she thinks. No more blaming Jacki for being born.

Gran smiles at Jack. She says his name. She takes his hand. And, once again, she is dancing. Dancing around her overheated bedroom, through the snibbed door, down the hall, out into the yard, above the long grass.

Keeping in perfect step, Gran and Jack are dancing a slow waltz—*one two three, one two three*—across the top of the thistle and grass, beneath the hooded sky.

Drive

One

My head hurts. I cover my ears, but the scream does not stop. It reverberates inside my head. It is the sound of the floor tiles screaming up at Michelle from beneath her bare feet. She has been sitting on the toilet, staring down at the tiles, for so long that the pattern—two smaller circles atop a much larger circle—has metamorphosed into a wide-eyed, open-mouthed, primal-scream choir.

The choir screams at Michelle loud enough for me to hear.

Michelle's head hurts, too.

It is late.

She should be sleeping.

She has been pencilled in for the early start, covering the breakfast rush. She feels exhausted, but cannot sleep. Part of her doesn't want today to end, because then she'll have to deal with tomorrow. Yet again she will have to pick herself up, start all over.

Michelle's backside has molded itself to the toilet seat. Sitting there, she wishes she had pinched one of Brendan's magazines.

It would be better if she had something to read.

Two

Outside, the air is no fresher. As soon as Suzie pushes through the clinic's doors, beyond the range of the air-conditioners, the humidity of the night falls upon her. She looks for the sky, but there is none—just low grey clouds blanketing the stars. Suzie walks unsteadily between the cars, lies down in a bus shelter emblazoned with graffiti.

'You orright?' Toby asks.

Annette catches up, points at Suzie: 'She stabbed me in the face and swore at me in the doctor's surgery.'

Suzie tells Annette to piss off.

'You still pissed off with me?' Toby asks, confused.

'No. Not you.'

'Don't worry, I'll get you the money.'

'How?'

'I'm thinkin'.'

'Yeah? Think faster.'

'Blood sucker,' Annette hisses.

Suzie spits, 'I should've stabbed you in the heart.'

'You're just jealous cos I'm popular and you're not.'

'I'd rather be dead than popular.'

Toby steps back, concerned: 'What're you doing?'

'Nuthin'.'

'Who're you talkin' to?'

Suzie chews her thumbnail.

'You orright? You feelin' orright?'

'...m'self. I'm talkin' to m'self.'

'D'you wanna go back to the doctor?'

'No fucken way. She's gunna lock me up.'

'You sure?'

'Look—shuddup, orright? Jeez, I wouldn't have been belted if you hadn't been so piss-weak. You didn't do anything. Just stood still and waited for him to fucken hit you.'

Toby starts to plead his defence, but Suzie doesn't hang around to hear. She's already walking towards the freeway, hands in pockets, feet scuffing along the concrete.

'Where're you goin'?' Toby calls.

'Your place.'

'You're walkin' there?'

'Nah. I'm flyin'.'

Toby and Suzie walk past row after row of triple-front brick-veneer houses with neat lawns, and clean cars parked out front. Some houses have their sprinklers going full-pelt, chattering in the night, saturating their gardens before water restrictions are enforced. Suzie can smell the moisture in the air.

Toby kicks along behind, retrieving stray bottle tops and stones from the footpath; weighing each item carefully in his hand, as if gauging its value, before tossing each one, bouncing them off terracotta roofs. Annette is further behind Toby, catcalling and singing as she cartwheels along the centre of the road, placing her hands on the double white lines, kicking her Reebok cross-trainers into the sky, then landing in front of herself, back on her feet. Cars pass intermittently—speeding because it's late and police cars and speed cameras are sparse out here—whooshing a shadow either side of Annette's exquisitely executed cartwheels, their high-beam lights making Suzie squint and look away.

Suzie stops, waits for Toby to catch up.

'You sure you don't have a smoke?'

'Sorry.'

'Cigarettes're bad for you,' Annette says as she cartwheels past.

'Jeez,' Suzie flops down in a driveway, sits cross-legged. Toby stretches out beside her on his belly.

'I'm knackered,' he says.

'You just had a sleep.'

'Yeah. I had a dream—'

Suzie cuts him off: 'I don't dream.'

'Whaddaya do when y'sleep, then?'

'How should I know? I close my eyes—an' when I open them it's morning.'

'Dreamin' about nuthin' is still dreamin'.'

'Bullshit.'

A car careers past, heading for the freeway overpass. Suzie looks around, but can't see Annette.

'What're you thinkin' about?' Toby asks out of the blue.

'Oh...you'n'your mum,' Suzie fibs.

'Yeah? What about her an' me?'

'She's orright, y'know? She's not like you, but.'

'Oh?'

'Yeah. You don't look like her. An' she's much more wound up than you, y'know? Like she's always ready to bolt. I was sitting in the car with her an' she was playin' with the windshield wipers, jigglin' her leg, rattlin' her keys. Couldn't help herself. But, you—it takes all my time just t'get you moving.'

Toby nods, 'Danny's like Mum...I'm gunna see him tomorrow and tell him about the bike.'

'It's fixed?'

'Nah. Not yet.'

'When can we go riding?'

'Soon.'

Suzie rubs the bandage on her forehead with the meat of her thumb, teases the pattern cut into her arm with her fingertips; wonders whether the stitches will leave a scar when removed. More scars the merrier, she thinks.

The razor is tucked away in Suzie's wallet. She has an urge to unwrap the white tissue again, vivisect herself. She wants to cut deeper than ever before. An idea rears in her head—unwrapping that razor again, slicing through the skin and flesh just above her bikini line with one slash, opening up her womb.

Shrinking from this image—I kick—I cry—I long to be held.

Suzie can hear the freeway nearby, just around the corner—traffic rushing to and from Another. Every weekday morning and evening, the freeway jams. Rush-hour commuters stew in their cars—driving into the morning sun on their way to work, driving into the evening sun on their way home.

Suzie rolls to her feet, slaps Toby on the shoulder: 'Lets go.'

'Where?'

'This way.'

She points towards the sound of the freeway.

'I'm buggered,' he protests.

'An' I need a smoke. Come on.'

The two of them follow the street as it swings around, runs beside the freeway along the length of the concrete barrier intended to muffle the traffic that merely amplifies the racket. Crossing the road, they trudge up the ramp of a pedestrian overpass. No one else is around.

The overpass is littered with cigarette butts and broken glass—a used syringe is discarded beside a rubbish bin. Suzie stops at the halfway point of the overpass, leans over the rail, watches the city-bound traffic hum directly beneath her. Her head reels. She pictures herself tipping over the rail, doing a belly flop onto the transit lane. *Jumpjumpjump*, Annette hums beside Suzie (inside Suzie). Toby says something to her, but seems an aeon away. Suzie bends over the rail, balances in the roar of wind and traffic—headlights blur by beneath her. Annette is bounding up and down the rail like a gymnast on the beam. She sticks a forward somersault right beside Suzie and puffs insistently, 'Jump!'

Just then, Toby grabs Suzie's arm. She pulls away violently, screams 'DON'T!'—causing Annette Norman to overbalance, slip wordlessly, sporting a petulent expression of impertinent disbelief, from the rail; inelegantly tumble down through the night into the well-lit path of a freeway bus. 'Fucken dobber cunt,' Suzie says.

Toby raises his hands in surrender: 'Sorry.'

She keeps looking over the rail at the freeway traffic, does not reply.

'Suzie?' Toby pleads.

She has an impulse to dive over the rail after Annette, finish the job.

'I'm sorry,' Toby says.

Suzie holds her breath for as long as she can, lets it out in a steady sigh. A cutaway image of her father's smiling mouth flickers in her head. After a long while she turns to Toby: looks at him as though he were a ghost.

'What is it?'

She shrugs: 'Nuthin'.'

'I thought you were gunna jump.'

'So?'

'So I grabbed you.'

'Well, y'shouldn't've.'

A truck roars directly beneath them—the overpass vibrates.

'Have you ever thought about it?' Suzie whispers.

Toby steps closer and lowers his voice, 'Killing myself?'

She nods.

He scratches the back of his neck: 'I've thought about it.'

'...and?'

'An' I'll be dead soon enough.'

Suzie puts her feet on the bottom of the rail, leans right over.

'Get down,' Toby pleads.

'D'you think I'm gunna jump now?'

'Dunno.'

Suzie gazes down upon the freeway: 'It looks pretty good from up here.'

He moves closer: 'Does it?'

'Better than good. Beautiful.'

'How d'you know?'

'What?'

'How d'you know it's beautiful? You've never been dead.'

'Nope.'

'So, how do you know if it's good or not?'

'Dead is dead is dead.'

'But, say I die in a car accident—right?—an' I'm thrown through the windscreen an' my head's cut clear off.'

'Yeah?'

'Well—what was the last thing I felt? Gettin' my head ripped off, right? So I could be like that forever, punching my head through a windscreen over an' over.'

'So, if I jumped right now, I'd fall forever?'

'I guess...I just think, yeah, life's shit, but who says the next life's not an even bigger shit? You'll be dead soon enough, so what's the rush?'

Suzie climbs down from the rail, gives Toby a level stare.

Three

The pedestrian overpass empties into a playground at the other side of the freeway.

'No monkey bars,' Suzie complains.

Toby clambers up, scuds down, the rusty slide. Suzie sits on the swing and, leaning against her own weight with her hands on the chain, slowly gathers momentum, becomes a human pendulum. The chain gives a metallic growl each time the swing reaches the end of its arc and starts to fall back to earth. Shadow children mill about, drawing in the sand, playing chasey: two boys balance on the seesaw, play king-of-the-castle, try to push each other off. Annette Norman is nowhere to be seen.

'The best playgrounds have monkey bars,' Suzie says.

'I like adventure playgrounds—they've got forts an' tunnels an' stuff,' Toby says.

'I like monkey bars.'

The swing growls.

'You hungry?' Toby asks. He is standing to one side, watching Suzie.

'I'm flyin',' she says.

Suzie launches herself into space and touches down perfectly in the sand.

Four

Michelle flushes the toilet, feels her way around the futon in the dark. Brendan has spread out diagonally—sprawling across her side of the bed as well as his own. Michelle finds a spare patch of futon and lies down, wedged between Brendan and the floor.

Michelle's shoulders sting from the sun and her mouth is dry.

She lies on her side.

She lies on her back.

She lies on her other side.

She lies on her back again.

'Fuck.'

Michelle gives up and reaches for her handbag, fishes out a cigarette and lighter, lights up and blows a long low cloud of white smoke into the black space above the futon.

Five

'What's this?'

'Our ride.'

'Whose car is it?'

'Who's car does it look like?'

Toby makes a deduction: 'Uh-huh.'

Suzie gives Toby's shoulder a shove: 'Go on.'

'What?'

'Do it.'

'Pinch it?'

'Yeah.'

'...I dunno.'

'Come on, Toby. We need a ride home. This is like public transport.'

Toby's sitting on the curb across from a block of units. Suzie's crouching behind him, whispering in his ear, chewing her nails. None of the neighbours' lights are on. There is no traffic. The street is quiet.

'I dunno.'

'Jeez, Toby.'

'What?'

'You're fucken chicken.'

'Am fucken not!'

'Come on. I got belted cos of you an' I got sacked cos of you.'

'Aw, fucken hell.'

Defeated, Toby gets up, walks across the road and up the units' communal driveway. Suzie stares hard into the darkness, straining her eyes to see what Toby is doing. Directly behind her, a soothing voice interrupts.

'Suzanne,' the voice says.

Suzie turns—and there's Just Rhonda sitting in her swivel chair behind her desk, hands clasped under her chin as though in prayer.

'You still haven't answered my question, Suzanne.'

'What question?'

'Why did you try to take your life?'

'Aw—fuck off.'

Just Rhonda tisks: 'Temper, temper.'

Suzie turns away, watches Toby in the drive.

'Suzanne?'

'What now?'

'You're avoiding my question. Self-mutilation, trying to kill yourself with a knife, threatening to jump onto the freeway. It's all a tad melodramatic don't you think?'

'You tell me.'

'Why, Suzanne? Why do you feel the need to do these things?'

'I dunno. Does there have to be a reason?'

'Nothing is without reason, Suzanne.'

Suzie shakes her head ruefully: 'I dunno 'bout that. I always think nothin' has reason.'

Six

Michelle pads into the bathroom: drops her cigarette into the toilet, where it expires with a hiss. The tiles are screaming beneath her bare feet, Michelle can feel them. Careful not to make a sound, keeping all the lights off, she checks all the rooms in the unit, ends up standing in the middle of the lounge.

Something's wrong. Something has Michelle's heart pounding in her ears.

She listens.

No noise. The rooms are heavy with warm stale air, the scent of Michelle's cigarettes and Brendan's body odour.

Michelle relaxes a notch. She is just about to give up and return to the bedroom when she hears a noise.

Someone's in the drive.

Michelle peeks between the dusty slats of the venetian blind. In the darkness she can see the outline of a man standing beside Brendan's car, trying to jimmy open the driver's door.

Suddenly aware of the fact that she is naked, Michelle covers her breasts with an arm as she watches the thief work. He is having trouble with the door. He is nervous, checking for trouble every few seconds. At one stage the thief glances at the lounge window, straight at Michelle, but it is dark—she cannot see his face, only shadow; and he cannot see her, only a venetian blind. Finally, he gets the door open, and on clicks the interior light. The thief slides behind the wheel, flicks off the light.

But not before Michelle sees Toby's face.

Seven

The back of Toby's neck—even the ridge of melted, scarred tissue—prickles with the expectation that, any second now, he'll be picked out by a spotlight in the sky. The spotlight will paralyze him, and, from above and behind the light a disembodied voice piped through a loudspeaker will order him to stop. Ask questions that demand answers.

Toby eases the bonnet down, snaps the dipstick off at the stem and runs back to the driver's side. The dipstick stub slots into the ignition. Toby fiddles, trying to turn over the ignition, but has no luck. He takes out the dipstick, pushes it back in; applying more pressure, twisting the dipstick repeatedly, until, finally, the steering wheel unlocks and the radio blares on. Jamming the radio off, Toby slots the car into neutral, unfastens the handbrake and steers awkwardly as the Honda rolls, arse-first, down the driveway. By the time the car rolls to a halt in the street, Suzie is at the passenger window tapping on the glass. Toby unlocks the door.

'About fucken time,' Suzie says.

'Fuck,' Toby mutters to himself.

'What now?'

The car won't start.

Toby is hunched over the steering wheel, frantically trying to coax the ignition to kick over.

'Suzanne,' Just Rhonda soothes from the back seat. 'Why don't we discuss what your father said?'

'Hurry up!' Suzie tells Toby.

'I am.'

'Hurry!'

'I am!'

'Your father says this is all about you being abandoned by your mother. Is that what you think?'

'Toby.'

'All your actions do seem to be a cry for help.'

'Toby!'

A naked man is sprinting down the driveway.

'Fucken hurry!' Suzie yells and ducks forward, burying her head between her knees. 'If he sees me we're ratshit.'

Toby hits the central locking.

'Hurry!'

'I am!'

Boompfh!—Brendan jumps onto the bonnet of his Honda, yelling and pounding on the roof. Toby keeps clicking the ignition as he stares down the barrel of Brendan's penis.

'Toby!' Suzie bawls.

The pounding and screaming is deafening. Toby pictures the spotlight—hovering, it is waiting for the perfect moment to pin him down.

'Park!'

'Huh?'

'Is it in park?!'

'Fuck.'

Toby slots the transmission from neutral into park. Tries again. This time the car roars into life.

'Dickhead,' Suzie growls.

The pounding on the roof intensifies as Toby floors the accelerator, feels his weight sink back into the bucket seat as the car propels itself towards the roundabout at the end of the street.

Once the car gathers speed the noise stops. Brendan is too busy hanging on, his deflated cock pressed flat against the windscreen like some squashed insect, to pound the roof. Squealing with glee, Suzie starts punching the section of the windscreen that Brendan's penis is pressed against. Toby, meanwhile, peers between Brendan's legs as he steers straight for the roundabout at speed. Easing off the accelerator, he slows to forty, waits until the car enters the intersection then hammers the brake, sending the car skidding. The Honda mounts the roundabout before it jags to a halt, throwing Brendan flying into a bed of tanbark.

'Dickhead!' Suzie screams as Toby slots Brendan's car into reverse, swings the Honda around and floors it for the freeway.

Eight

The world looks different from a speeding car.

Suzie rests her head on the window-sill, the breeze slapping her cheeks. Her left arm trails in the black silk night as the car cruises the freeway, speeds towards the hard left turn that feeds into Another. Toby has been zigzagging through suburban streets for the past hour—taking them past rows of cutout shapes, the shadowy fronts of so many three-bedroom houses.

At first, they are delirious.

'First time I seen Brendan outta his Maccas uniform,' Suzie says as she ransacks the glove box and the driver's console—searching hopefully for money or cigarettes, but only coming up with a dollar, in assorted five and ten cent pieces, and a packet of chewing gum. She pockets the change and munches hungrily on the chewies, shoving two and three at a time into her mouth to quell her nicotine craving.

Toby drives with one hand on the wheel, his elbow pointing into the breeze, just like Danny used to when he drove Mum's Kingswood.

Just Rhonda sits in the back, asking Suzie question after question about her mother, but Suzie pretends she doesn't hear.

After driving around for a while they wonder what to do next.

'We could do a smash'n'grab,' Suzie suggests.

'What's that?'

'I saw it on telly. People pinch cars, drive them through a shop window, steal stuff an' drive off.'

Toby shakes his head.

'How 'bout we drive up to Surfer's Paradise. Go an' see my mum.'

'I thought your mum was in Hollywood.'

'She is. But she flies down there sometimes for holidays an' stuff. Y'know, just to take it easy.'

'Is that what you really believe?' Just Rhonda asks.

'We don't have enough juice to drive to Surfers. No money, neither,' Toby says.

Toby pulls up in a side street, motor running, gets out and pisses against a tree. Suzie stretches her legs—standing, hands in pockets, jiggling her ill-gotten change.

'Y'know, I'll prob'ly have a scar when they take the stitches out.'

'Yeah,' Toby zips himself up.

'I'd like another scar.'

Toby wipes his hands on Danny's overalls.

'I want you to give me a scar.'

Toby walks back to the car, ignoring Suzie's request, so she repeats it.

'I heard,' Toby says. He shuts the driver's door with a hard tug.

After that pit stop they drive fast. Toby steering with both hands on the wheel, taking the racing line through the suburban streets as he cuts from one side of the road to the other. Suzie, window wound down, letting the wind slap her in the face.

Eventually, the streets empty onto the freeway. Here, Toby drives faster still—passing other cars as though they're standing still—until they leave the traffic behind.

The wind slips through Suzie's outstretched fingers. She closes her eyes. Hypnotised by the white lines, Toby relaxes, takes a hand off the wheel.

They speed past a police cruiser parked beneath an overpass, but don't notice until it pulls out, blue-and-cherry lights blazing.

'Cops,' Toby says—gripping the wheel with both hands.

Suzie spins in her seat.

'I'm here if you want to talk,' Just Rhonda says to her.

Toby hesitates for a beat, then floors it. The lights are half a kilometre behind them, gaining fast. The end of the freeway is approaching. And an image flits through Toby's mind—Danny flying through the air, backlit by a brilliant yellow canvas—but is overtaken by the momentum of the car.

'Faster!' Suzie says.

She is swivelled around, watching the incandescent blue-and-cherry lights bloom, loom larger until they fill the rear window, until the sound of the siren fills the Honda.

The cruiser's headlights are on high beam: the white light bouncing off the rear-view mirror, branding a slit across the bridge of Toby's nose and bloodshot eyes.

The end of the freeway is dead ahead—a bank of warning signs and black and white arrows pointing hard to the left.

Toby brakes hard, turns late into the corner—and the image of Danny wearing his leathers, suspended against the yellow canvas of the sky, returns; fills Toby's mind. It is all he sees as he slides into the corner—tyres tearing at the black bitumen as they fight to maintain traction. When Toby's eyes clear he is driving down Another's main drag on the wrong side of the road—the interior of the Honda pulsating electric blue-and-cherry shadows, vibrating from the siren's wail. Suzie is gripping the dashboard, laughing crazily—her teeth pink, then purple, from the lights. They have already passed the servo and are about to pass McDonald's when Toby thinks better of it—wrenching the car into a fishtail of a right hand turn.

The underbelly of the Honda hits the curb hard, slowing them, bouncing them into the air. They pummel across the nature strip, scrape Suzie's passenger door against a brick wall as they crash through the Drive-Thru. Toby eases off to keep the car in a straight line, then, once they have cleared the brick wall, guns the accelerator—sending the car leaping forward and to the left, flattening the ORDER HERE microphone box, narrowly missing the menu board.

The police cruiser overshoots the Honda's hard right—has to slow and turn round before it can resume the chase.

'Faster!' Suzie yells gleefully.

Aiming for the paddock at the far end of the car park, Toby bounces over parking bays, over the concrete curb where he and Suzie sat eating free Quarter Pounders—crashing through the wire fence, ploughing into the long grass paddock, scattering shadows left, right and centre. Part of the fence catches under the car, making it veer right as it ricochets over the hard-baked earth. Driving blind, the car gradually loses its momentum and speed.

Toby checks the rear-view mirror. There are no blue-and-cherry lights. He brakes, sending the Honda shuddering to a halt.

'Fuck!' Suzie yells as she head-butts the windshield. The shadow of Just Rhonda sails between the front seats, passes through the windshield without shattering it, and disappears into the night.

Toby jumps out and runs round to Suzie, flings her door open.

'You orright?'

Suzie is dazed—fresh blood has seeped through her white bandage.

He helps her into the maze of long grass.

Nine

The police helicopter concentrates along Another's rear fence line: patrolling back and forth, flooding the backyards and paddocks with white light. Toby and Suzie lie in the grass, waiting for a break. Toby is on top of Suzie, smothering her light blouse with Danny's leather jacket as the chopper hovers directly above—its cabin tilted forward, slicing through the heat, making the air vibrate with its twin engines and rotor blades.

Toby can see the giant blue-and-white bird with *Police* stencilled on its fuselage and a St John ambulance insignia tattooed to the side door. Suzie is shaking. At first Toby thinks she is crying, but when she rolls over she's laughing—her face flushed, her bandage swollen with blood.

The chopper passes over, and Suzie and Toby run for the back fence, slip into the Purcell's house through the kitchen door. Inside, Suzie hoists herself onto the kitchen bench, Toby rummages through the fridge.

'I'm starvin',' he moans.

'I wanna smoke.'

'You're not hungry?'

She shrugs: 'What's to eat?'

'Nuthin'. Just eggs, cheese an' milk—an' some lettuce.'

'No bread?'

Toby opens the cupboard, produces a half-eaten loaf of white bread and they start toasting. After pouring themselves two tall lime cordials, Toby and Suzie sit at the table and polish off the loaf. Toby eats four slices smeared with margarine and peanut butter. Suzie dawdles over a piece of marmalade toast, then abandons a second slice after a bite. Toby eyes off Suzie's last piece of toast until she pushes her plate across the table, then he wolfs it down. They then sit, glug their cordials, listen for the chopper.

Suzie speaks first: 'I'd kill for a smoke.'

'You're like a broken record.'

'Are there any around?'

'Doubt it.'

Suzie rummages through cupboards and drawers, systematically ransacking the kitchen, then the lounge and, finally, the bedrooms. Toby leans back—making his chair stand on its hind legs until the back of his head rests against the wall.

'Michelle's the only one who still smokes,' he calls.

'What?'

'Gran isn't allowed to anymore an' Mum's quit. Michelle might have some in her room.'

'Which room?'

'The one at the end of the hall.'

'The one with the lock?' her voice floats back.

'That's Gran.'

Suzie studies the snib lock, which has been slid across the doorjamb and fastened. She cannot help thinking about burnt shoes, about how the smell of the plastic and leather had stung her nostrils, had made it painful to breathe. Suzie touches the silver metal of the snib lock. Her hand recoils, as though burnt...in her mind's eye, she was standing out by the incinerator again. Suzie had just touched one of her mother's burnt patent leather shoes—the black ones with the low heels which Suzie had clunked up and down the coffee table in, imagining herself a catwalk model, earning herself a crisp slap across her bare legs.

The sting of her mother's slap—the exhilaration and alarm—is still vivid for Suzie: she has cut away every other memory of physical contact.

The burnt shoes had been curled in on themselves; the leather shrunk by the incinerator's trained heat. Touching the shoe, the radiating heat had shocked Suzie. She had fetched a stick. Mrs Collier had come outside and told Suzie to be careful, but Suzie had started screaming and waving the stick, forcing her to retreat to the kitchen. She had held her ground until her Dad came home from work and gave her so many bruises she had to steal a kitchen knife to try to cut them all out.

The next room along from Gran's is deserted. Door and cupboards are flung open; the bed stripped; wire hangers, plastic shopping bags, empty shoe boxes and scraps of shopping receipts, and one and two cent pieces, are strewn across the carpet, which is worn down to the weave in some places. The battered dresser is empty, containing only the odd bobby pin or bus ticket; except for the bottom drawer. Suzie pulls it open and inside finds a dog-eared copy of *Your Wedding* magazine—featuring a cover shot of a bride modelling a raw silk number, an old Lady Di-style gown. The face of the cover model had been meticulously cut out with nail scissors. Suzie flicks through the magazine. Every other face of every other model bride had been clipped out, too.

Toby is fiddling with the dead TV. Suzie returns from Michelle's room, lies on the couch.

'No luck?'

'No smokes,' she says. 'But I got some money.'

She produces a handful of change.

'Where'd y'get the shrapnel?'

'Your mum's undies drawer.'

Suzie empties her pockets onto the carpet—gets down on her hands and knees to add up their ill-gotten change.

'Fuck!' Toby swears at the TV.

'Shuddup. You're makin' me lose count,' Suzie says, counts aloud, 'Two thirty, two forty, two sixty, two seventy-five. There.'

Toby's still wrestling with the TV.

'Kick it again. Maybe that'll work.'

'Very funny.'

Toby pokes around the back of the TV some more; switching switches and unplugging plugs.

'I just need a couple more bucks for some smokes,' Suzie moans.

'No way,' Toby interjects.

'What?'

'We need that for the bus.'

'Bullshit. This's nearly half a packet of smokes.'

'I gotta see Danny.'

'Why d'you have to see him?'

'Cos, orright? He's m'brother.'

Suzie slumps back into the couch, sulks for a while, chewing her nails, then remembers to tell Toby that Michelle's room is empty.

'Empty?'

'Yep. She move out?'

'Who gives a shit?...There.'

He tries switching the TV on again. Nothing.

'Fuck.'

'Pinch another telly.'

'They're too big to shoplift.'

Toby crawls over to the couch, lies on top of Suzie.

'Whadda you want?'

'Sleep,' he says.

'Know what I want?'

'What?'

'A hundred bucks.'

'Oh—I thought you where gunna say a smoke.'

'I'm rooted without the money, but.'

'Yep.'

'So whadda we gunna do?'

'You could stay here for a while.'

Suzie wriggles out from under Toby, onto the carpet. Looks at him for a long while.

'Orright, then,' she finally says.

Ten

On the way to the van, Toby stops in the garage; swings the door up, finds the switch in the dark. The fluorescent tube stutters before filling the room with harsh white light.

Suzie walks past Toby to the dismembered Yamaha. It is laid out in pieces on the blue plastic sheet—both wheels taken off, laid in a nest of mangled spokes, the front tyre stripped so Toby can hammer the rim straight; the broken chain snaked into a question mark; the mirror, a petrol cap, triangles of Perspex, are arranged in the corner of the plastic sheet closest to Suzie. She drops to one knee, picks up the mirror that's been snapped off at the stem like a chrome flower. She asks Toby if she can keep it.

'Why?'

'Cos I like it.'

'But it's useless.'

'But I like it.'

He sinks his hands into his pockets. She holds the mirror close: it is pock-marked with rust, grubby with fingerprints.

'I like it,' she repeats.

'It's Danny's,' Toby says. 'Not mine to give.'

'What? I can't have it?'

'It's not mine. It's Danny's.'

'So's that leather jacket. So's those overalls. Take 'em off.'

'Suzie.'

'Orright, then. I'll just have to ask Danny, then.'

Eleven

It is not a matter of choice. It is a matter of strength. And Suzie is the stronger. I see them kill the garage lights—walk out into the darkness trailed by a shadow carrying a gun and a jerry can.

Suzie stops. Toby stands at her side in the junk yard. She half turns and kisses him on the mouth. I feel the rush of blood to his face, his groin. She leads him by the hand into the caravan, to the bunk bed, undresses him brusquely, pushes him onto the bed. He lies obediently while she roots around the caravan for a knife and matches, before returning and lighting a half-spent candle on the floor beside the bed.

Standing in the candlelight, she unbuttons her Maccas tunic, shows him where she wants a scar, takes the knife and carves a shape in the air for illustration. Toby shakes his head, but knows he cannot refuse Suzie.

They argue while she undresses. He contending that he cannot hurt her, she replying that he can if he has her permission. He arguing that he doesn't want to, she insisting that what he wants is beside the point. 'I want you to,' she says, 'and that should be enough.' He confessing that he is scared, she telling him to be brave. They talk back and forth until she is perfectly naked: a bruised, milk-white angel.

She climbs onto the bed, straddles him, with his chest between her knees, and kisses him lightly—tells him to be quiet.

The inside of the caravan is more shadow than light—the candle's yellow flame casts mottled shadows against the wall and low ceiling. Suzie is lying on top of Toby, covering his nakedness with hers. When her body rises from his, Suzie can see his scars—in the candlelight his skin appears molten, like freshly melted wax.

'Inside petals first,' Suzie whispers as she rolls onto her back.

Toby kneels over her, heats the point of his pocket knife, the one with the imitation pearl handle, in the candle flame. Suzie rubs his back, his sides, with the heels of her hands. Toby sits, holding the heated knife, staring at the candle flame.

'What is it?' Suzie asks.

'I don't wanna hurt you.'

'You won't.'

'Course I will.'

'Look, Toby, this is nuthin'. Gettin' a nose job's much worse.'

'Why?'

'Well—it hurts more. They knock you out and break your nose. You look like someone's kicked y'face in.'

Toby gives a doltish nod.

Suzie continues, 'An' it's dangerous, too. Get this. I read about this woman who had a nose job an' went blind. They reckoned the nose job bled into her eyes, or somethin'. So she's got a nice new nose, but she can't see it. So, guess what happens next?'

Toby fondles the pocket knife as Suzie talks.

'This woman's gotta daughter, hasn't she? And she sees her mum's blind, but goes, *Oh, whatta nice nose*. An' she gets a nose job, too...So, now they're both blind.'

The pocket knife is warm in Toby's hands. He takes the knife from the candle flame and starts carving—beginning with the inside petal, working his way out.

Sharp and hot—the blade cauterizes as it carves into the milk skin.

Suzie lies still, but wraps her thighs around his trunk and squeezes hard.

Toby is sweating. Aroused, yet alarmed.

The rose is a red bud between Suzie's breasts.

He rubs his face with his free hand—finger-paints his nose and cheeks with Suzie's blood—then holds the knife over the candle until the tip of the blade turns black.

Morning

One

The wick of the candle drowned in its own wax just before sunrise. A ribbon of smoke twirled into the air, twined itself above where Toby and Suzie lay sleeping.

Toby's dream is smoke. Smoke that is cut adrift in an early morning that is without breeze. Barely lighter than air, Toby floats slowly, rests against the ceiling of the van—beneath him are two naked forms, entwined: separate torsos bonded by the mortar of sleep, wax, oil, coagulated blood.

Suzie's rose is black with dried blood. The lips of her petals pout, tender to humidity and touch: a tortured flower of bruised and burnt flesh, broken skin, blackened blood.

The rose is alive. It is growing—a carnivore fed on blood and bone.

Two

Sunrise. Streaks of shadow stretch across the car park as Mum cuts across Shoppingtown's empty bays. She is walking briskly because she is tired, in a rush to get home. The morning air is dry and ominously still, warning of another day of debilitating heat. As she walks, Mum ignores the ache in her shoulders and lower back, the stiffness in her knees. The first of the day workers are arriving—picking out the shaded parks, draping towels over steering wheels, fitting sunshades across windscreens, brushing past Mum. The men wearing ironed pants, shirts and ties. The women: skirts and blouses.

In her tracksuit pants and T-shirt, Mum feels frumpy, invisible. She runs a hand through her hair, sending a sharp pain down her spine and legs, right to the backs of her knees.

Nearing the Kingswood, Mum's pace slows, stops. The Kingswood has been vandalized. Bright yellow shapes—letters reading No Slopes—are spray-painted along the driver's side of the car.

Mum stands there with the morning sun hard in her face, squinting. She reads the graffiti. Reads the words aloud, as though asking a question. Touches the yellow letters. Feels the car's hot metal skin.

Three

Shadows dance across the Kingswood's cracked windscreen as Mum trawls home, sitting just below a hundred, eyeing the engine temperature. The car runs hot in summer, tends to overheat in heavy traffic or if it is driven too hard, so, although she wants to flog the car, Mum reigns herself in—the last thing she needs is a cooked motor.

Turned low, the radio buzzes with static. This far out of the city the frequency breaks up, is never perfect, but Mum doesn't notice, can barely hear the radio interference over the drone of the engine.

Pulling hard on the wheel, she follows the freeway as it veers away from the hazard signs, funnels into the main drag of Another.

Four

Suzie does not dream.

Instead, she sinks into herself, beneath her broken milk skin and bruised flesh, into her very marrow; becoming the blood rushing through her veins, feeding her rose scar.

I feel Suzie.

Her blood roars in my ears.

Her anger burns within me.

Five

McDonald's is a shambles. Skid marks swerve through the Drive Thru, which is cordoned off. Muddled with fatigue, Mum drives into the Drive Thru lane, pulls up to where the ORDER HERE contraption used to be, but is flummoxed to find a fibreglass stump. Then she notices the CLOSED sign on the Menu board.

Mum parks, hears her knees click as she stands, sees the black skid marks leading down from the ORDER HERE stump to the car park to the broken fence line. A corridor has been mown into the paddock, through the long grass and thistle.

Walking towards the restaurant, Mum spots a police cruiser parked outside the servo—instinctively thinks of Toby.

Inside, plastic flowers and paper place-mats featuring cottage garden prints are set out on the laminated tabletops—the air is chilled, air-conditioned. A smattering of businessmen, wet hair combed back from their foreheads, are spaced out around the window seats—tucking into hot cakes, McMuffins, hash browns, and Big Breakfasts; reading the free newspapers.

Mum stops, blinks, when she sees who is standing behind the counter.

It's Michelle—wearing a brand spanking new McDonald's uniform.

Michelle's mouth opens, closes, when she spots Mum.

'Hi Mum,' she says.

'Hello there,' Mum replies coolly.

'Can I take your order?'

'My order? Oh, yes...I'll have a coffee and a muffin.'

'Would you like a hash brown?'

'No, dear. Thank you.'

Michelle dawdles over the register, hunts for the right keys to peck, then hustles off to fill the order. Brendan is hobbling around in the kitchen.

'What happened to the Drive-Thru?' Mum asks as Michelle pours her coffee.

'Do you want cream with that?'

'Ta,' Mum says.

'Sugar?'

'Ta...So, what happened here last night?'

Michelle clips a plastic lid onto the coffee cup, collects the milk and sugar containers and puts them on a tray, says in a rush: 'Someone stole Brendan's car and ran over the Drive-Thru box, okay?'

'Who's Brendan?'

'The manager.'

'Oh.'

Michelle calls 'McMuffin!' and idles by the food warmer until Brendan slides a paper parcel down the McMuffin slide. She returns to the counter, plonks the parcel on Mum's tray.

'That'll be one-seventy,' Michelle says.

Mum pops a two-dollar coin in her hand, says: 'Nice to see you've finally got a job, then.'

Michelle bristles: 'What d'you mean?'

'Nuthin'. Just that it's good, that's all, you gettin' a job. Pity it didn't happen a long time ago.'

'I've had jobs before.'

'Last year. You're a bit old for Maccas, aren't cha? I thought they got 'em straight out of primary school.'

'Brendan says it's never too late to start a new career.'

'Oh,' Mum gushes sarcastically. 'So it's Brendan says, is it? Good friend of yours, this Brendan, is he?'

Michelle punches a key and the cash register slams open. She counts out thirty cents, slaps the change on Mum's tray.

Six

Michelle never went back to Safeway. How could she? John was in hospital, Danny had seventeen stitches in his head; and Michelle knew, just knew, that all the girls—Cindy, Kelly, and especially Josephine—would blame her for what happened at the nightclub. First they'd blame Danny, then her. They'd call Danny an animal, ask Michelle how she could stay with him after what he did, and, when she didn't walk away from Danny, they'd turn on her—start talking about her, calling her bitch or scrag to her face or, even worse, behind her back.

Michelle couldn't bear the thought of it—the confrontation—so she never went back. She sat at home and, for the first few weeks, harboured a forlorn hope that one of the girls—Cindy, she was the kindest—would drop by to see how she was going, but that hope was never realized. Nobody came. Michelle sat at home watching the TV with Danny and Gran, ate herself out of her little black dress, started talking about how much she wanted to be a hairdresser.

Danny told Michelle he liked the weight she'd put on, and that he liked her being at home. He started working in the backyard on his under-the-table panel-beating jobs—charging five hundred to fix a front-end that a bloke'd been quoted a thousand for, then pocketing the difference. 'Easy money,' he'd tell Michelle. 'Everyone makes money 'cept for the fucken insurance company.' Michelle'd sit out in the garage and watch him work sometimes. Danny was happiest working a car: popping a bent door back into place, redoing the duco so that it looked brand new or, as he liked to brag, 'better'n brand new.'

Better than brand new. Danny liked living in a world were he had the power to bend anything back into shape, fix his mistakes. Whenever he hit Michelle he'd get upset, apologize, then start playing doctor: cleaning up the mess, talking in a warm, paternal manner as he doled out instructions: 'Let's see now... Put Mum's Kiwi cream on in the morning and at night. That should clear up the cigarette burn. But don't wash the dishes for a couple of days, getting it wet could make it septic.'

'Michelle!' Brendan calls from the kitchen.

She is day-dreaming at the counter.

'Michelle!'

'What?' Michelle turns round.

Brendan has come out to the front counter area; favouring one leg as he stands, hands on hips. 'What're you doing?'

'Waiting on customers.'

'Waiting's more like it. Go out and refill their coffees.'

Michelle takes the coffee pot, grazes around the restaurant, topping up coffee cups. Mum's table is the last table she reaches.

'More coffee?'

Flashing a regal smile, Mum holds out her coffee cup, asks, 'Are you screwing this Brendan fella?'

Michelle splashes coffee on the floor. 'Shit.'

'So—you are fucking him.'

'That's none of your fucken business.'

'Danny's business is my business.'

'My business is my business.'

Steamed, Michelle returns to the counter, clunks the coffee pot onto its hotplate, watches Mum take her time over that free second cup of coffee.

Bitch, she thinks. Fucken bitch. I shoulda told the cops about Toby. The bitch wouldn't be so smug then.

Mum finishes her coffee, waves to Michelle as she leaves. Michelle clears off Mum's table, stands there, stewing, as customers congregate at the front counter.

'Service!' Brendan calls from the kitchen.

She doesn't move.

'Michelle!'

Everyone in the queue stares at Michelle. Brendan swears under his breath, hobbles around to take orders. Michelle turns, takes in the faces of the customers—their mouths crammed with half-chewed hot cakes, hash browns and McMuffins—and runs for the door.

Seven

Mum's Kingswood pulls into the drive. Gravel crunches beneath the worn tread of its tyres. The engine turns over—dies. The handbrake rips on, the door slams with a clunk, the car ticktickticks as its metal begins to cool, contract.

The noise—double concussions of the car door slamming, followed by the front door—brings Suzie to the brink of consciousness. Her eyelids flutter. Her beautiful, bruised body turns in its sleep, hits the floor of the caravan with a thud. And she is awake.

Mum paces around the house. Up and down the hall, in and out of Michelle's abandoned room; clattering about the bathroom cabinet, looking for a painkiller and a hair-band—but Michelle's cleaned everything out.

'Shit.' Mum stamps her foot. Finally, she goes to the kitchen, ties her hair back with a rubber band. It pinches her scalp. 'Shit-a-brick.' There are dishes in the sink and crumbs on the kitchen table. 'Tow-bee.' She wonders whether he brought her good towel back from the doctor's. From the kitchen, she can see the van; its door is wide open—he must be home. A noise—*Beepbeep! Beepbeep!*—reverberates from inside the van, which reminds Mum of Suzie—the milk-pale girl. She wonders how old that Suzie girl is, whether her parents know what she's up to. I should call 'em, she thinks. But I can't remember her last name. Can't be buggered.

Suzie scrounges through a pile of clothes on the floor until she finds the mobile.

The SMS reads: **I'VE CALLED THE POLICE & REPORTED U MISSING. IF UR NOT MISSING U WILL WISH U WERE. DAD.**

'Liar,' Suzie says.

'What?' Toby's sleepy head half rises off the pillow.

'Nuthin'. Go back to sleep.'

Mum unsnibs the lock, steps into Gran's room, which is dim and stuffy. For an instant, she thinks Gran is asleep.

Gran is lying very still, but she is not sleeping. Lying on her back, crocheted beanie pulled over her head, she stares at the ceiling with glass eyes.

Mum is not sure what she is supposed to do next. She steals across the carpet, kneels with her elbows on the mattress, studies Gran's petrified profile. Long ago, Gran's skin lost the elasticity of youth. It is loose, sagging at the cheeks and jowls, pulling her face and lips out of shape. Mum wonders what Gran looked like before she was Gran, back when she was young. Or was she ever young? Mum kneels beside her mother's body, staring hard, trying to picture Gran before Pa bent her nose out of shape. Gran has always seemed the same ancient bitter relic to Mum, even before she got sick.

The only time Mum ever saw Gran dolled up—face made up, hair permed—was at Pa's funeral. Gran looked a treat. She lashed out, bought a brand new frock—a pale blue number with a frilly collar—and slashed bright red lipstick over her mouth and a lick of blue eye shadow above each eye. 'Shouldn't we wear black?' Mum suggested. Gran bared teeth smeared with blood-red lipstick. 'Speak for y'self,' she said. Gran clipclopped down to the church in an old pair of heels she'd pulled out of the back of her cupboard. A smattering of people showed up at the church—mostly the wrecks Pa drank with down at the pub. Mum kept an eye on Gran throughout the ceremony and at the graveside. She couldn't take her eyes off the gaudy figure wobbling around on her high-heels, checking her hair in windows, acting like she was expecting a late arrival to come waltzing through the door. As the day wore on, though, Gran's made-up face began to fracture—the blue eyeliner frayed around the edges of her eyes, the red lipstick bled into the crevices of her face.

Suzie can't see her rose properly. It's too low and there are no mirrors in Toby's van. With a light touch, she pets the rose, pulls on her bloodied blouse; goes out and crouches in the sandbox to piss.

A jumbo lumbers overhead, descending from the sky. Suzie scratches under her arms, wonders vaguely whether her real mother's aboard the jumbo, whether she can see her daughter from so far up...but stops wondering when she hears the police divisional van come up the gravel drive, park behind Mum's Kingswood.

She streaks back to the van.

Eight

The divi-van swings into the drive, brakes hard—making something locked in its cage *Thump!* against the back of the driver's cabin as it slides to a halt. The racket starts up as soon as the van's engine shuts off—a yelling and pounding coming from inside the cage. Mum's standing on the front steps, not wanting to sit inside with Gran. An outline of a thin face presses against the wire-and-glass window, sees Mum, yells something incomprehensible.

A senior constable with a red face, lurid scratches that curl up from the corners of his mouth, and a huge moustache, hurls himself from the driver's seat, hammers on the roof of the divi-van with a meaty paw.

'Shut it!' he orders. 'Shut it! Orright? Or I'll shut it for you.'

'Fuck you!' a muffled voice howls back.

The constable hammers again, 'One more peep, sonny, just one more an' you'll know all about it.'

Mum has migrated from the steps to the drive. She stands, arms-folded, in front of the divi-van as it wheezes hot air through its grill.

'Nuthin' t'worry about,' the constable tells Mum. 'Just some skinhead I picked up this morning. Quite the artist. He was spray-painting racist graffiti on the side of a house. Pretty fucken bright, this one. Didn't even see me pull up behind him'—he hammers the roof—'did you, genius? He couldn't even spell ASIANS right, dumb shit...Anyway, that's not what we're here for. An ambulance is on the way, but I heard the call and thought I should check in. Can I see the deceased?'

Mum leads the policeman into Gran's bedroom. He clicks his tongue.

'Yep. She's deceased,' he says blandly. 'Relation of yours I take it?'

'My mother.'

'Condolences,' he says with a curt nod, then barges on, 'Right. So, you're the one who made the call, then'—he checks his notebook—'Mrs Purcell?'

'Jacki Purcell.'

'Hello, Jacki,' the constable says. 'I'm Senior Constable Finch.'

Mum takes Finch out to the kitchen. He sits in Toby's chair, back to the wall, and, as Mum puts on the kettle, wipes down the table with a sponge, fingers the raw scratches on his face, asks cursory questions about Gran, all the while scribbling in his notebook with a black pen.

Mum is wary. She doesn't like the police—they're more trouble than they're worth. When Gary was beating the shit out of her, the cops never lifted a finger, but, as soon as Toby or Danny stepped out of line, they swooped, hauling the boys off to the Children's Court, then the Magistrates' Court.

Finch changes the subject, asks Mum whether she has any kids.

'Me?'

Finch gestures to the empty room as if to say, Who else?

'Two boys.'

'Two boys. Great—me, I've got three kids. A boy and two girls—little tackers.'

The kettle starts squealing. Mum makes two instant coffees in mismatched mugs.

'Ta,' Finch says.

He waits until Mum sits back down again, then asks for Toby and Danny's names.

'You want their names?'

Finch smiles—a smile accentuated by Suzie's scratch marks—and says, 'Yes, please. I love names.'

'Danny and Toby,' Mum concedes.

'Danny and Toby, eh? Great. An' they're both still at home?'

Mum's mug hits the table hard, slopping coffee.

'Careful there, Jacki,' Finch says and sips his own coffee. 'D'you work nightshift, Jacki? I used to. Just switched to mornings a month ago. It's much better. I get to see the kids at night, y'know, take 'em to Macca's, keep tabs on them...It's important to know what y'kids're doing, Jacki.'

Mum's mug steams. Beneath the tabletop her hands start picking at each other.

'So, Jacki. Where's Toby?' Finch is leaning forward, leaning so far across the table that Mum can smell him—stale sweat and nicotine.

'What's he done?'

Finch's smile broadens, 'He's caught my eye, Jacki. That's what he's done. Toby's got a record, hasn't he? Breaking and entering, isn't it? Well he's obviously been looking to expand his resume, cos he's out spray-painting cars with my skinhead right now. And, last night, two kids—a boy and a girl—stole a car, parked it nearby. And Toby's girlfriend—what's her name? Suzanne Collier?—well, her parents have reported her missing. Not to mention the fact that there was another break-and-enter in a house nearby. Do you see a pattern here, Jacki? Your son has caught my eye. Now where is he?'

'I took them both to the doctor last night. Someone beat them up.'

Finch chuckles, 'And where's Toby now?'

'Dunno.'

'Bullshit, Jacki! Course you know. Where's his room?'

'In the caravan.'

'The caravan, eh? Let's go see, then.'

There's no stalling. Finch strides straight out the back door, through the yard, and bounces into the van. He is back out in the yard—sweating—by the time Mum catches up.

'Jeez, it stinks in there,' he complains. 'Didn't you teach your kid to clean up after himself?'

Nine

Toby has black spots in his eyes from staring into the heart of the sun. He blinks, blinks again, but the colour—a canvas of brilliant yellow—is still there: a canvas of colour burnt into his mind.

Danny.

Toby jolts in his seat, but Suzie doesn't notice. The bus rolls too much on its lazy suspension for her to notice. It makes her queasy, all that rocking. She chews her nails furiously, keeps her hands occupied, as the bus hauls along the freeway—its interior flooded with the whiff and din of its diesel engine.

Suzie stops chewing her nails, yells at Toby: 'I'd kill for a smoke!'

Although he only comprehends the last word—smoke—Toby is by now familiar enough with the sentiment. He nods sympathetically.

Suzie is weather-beaten. Unwashed, pale and bruised, her right eye socket a bloom of blue-black skin, sweating because she's wearing Danny's leather jacket to cover her bloodied blouse, Suzie begs strangers for cigarettes.

The languid heat of the bus makes Toby drowsy. He leans against Suzie, smells the leather jacket, thinks of his brother.

Ten

Standing alone in the drive, images of Danny wash over Mum.

...Danny playing in the dirt as a toddler while young Jacki watched from the back step...Danny watching his father yell and scream and kick and punch his pregnant mother... Danny looking after the baby when Jacki was too battered to crawl out of bed...Danny bullying little Toby, echoing his father...Danny on the night of the fire, brandishing a kitchen knife... Danny visiting Toby's blistered body in the hospital...Danny growing lean and hard and dark...

She does not know what she could have done to make things turn out different, doesn't know where she could have started.

Jacki tried.

She took the boys and the car, ran for all their lives. She'd always known she had to escape from Gary, but waited, hoping her life would heal itself. Every time he came down too hard, Gary'd drive her home from Gran's place, say how he didn't mean it, say how he loved her and the kids; and everything would be better, quieter, for a while. Jacki'd kid herself that it was all over with, that the last beating really was the last—but it never was.

The trigger for Jacki was when Ringo *the dog* turned out to be Ringo *the bitch*, and gave birth to a mongrel litter of five pups in the middle of the backyard. Jacki washed the five puppies in a bucket of warm water, put out an old mat for them to lie on beside their mother. That was the summer Jacki was pregnant with Toby. She sat on the back step, watching Ringo licking and nuzzling her puppies. Danny poured milk into a saucer, which they lapped up hungrily.

Jacki was cooking tea when Gary came home from work. She heard the puppies yapping, caught a glimpse of Gary through the kitchen window—striding up the drive with a wheel-jack in his fist. Jacki heard the puppies yelping—then a crunch—and they were howling, screaming. Breathless, wanting to throw up, Jacki ran down the steps, across the ragged lawn to where Gary stood, one foot on the bloody mat, clubbing the puppies with the flat end of the jack. Blank-faced, Danny stood to the side, watching the killing.

Jacki threw herself at Gary, but he clouted her across the shoulder with the jack—sending her flying to the dirt. That distraction gave Ringo enough of an opening to bite Gary's hand, make him even more murderous.

Jacki lay in the dirt, crying, as Gary's arm rose and fell, bringing the jack down until the yelping stopped; leaving just the sound of the blows, metal breaking bone. By the time the noise stopped Gary was splattered with blood and sweat.

Mum sees the blood again, hears the dogs scream; remembers how Danny was, afterwards. The boy had seen it all, stood there with his hands pressed to his ears—but still watching—as his father killed the dogs. *Blank.*

The boy was blank.

Did not speak a word.

Did not blink an eye.

Two men in dark blue uniforms brush past Mum, lift the gurney down the steps. It all seems pointless, the two paramedics taking ridiculous care not to jar Gran. She is strapped into the gurney, still wearing her beanie: eyes open, stone dead.

Mum watches them carry Gran over the gravel drive, past the divi-van, load her into the back of the ambulance.

Finch walks up, tells Mum to call him when Toby turns up. She just looks at him.

'It'll be better for everyone that way,' he says. 'Believe me, Jacki.'

The ambulance leaves first, driving away without the fanfare of its sirens. Finch follows—hurtling down the drive backwards, swinging the divi-van's arse around when he hits the street, slotting it into first, then putting his foot to the floor. Mum hears the skinhead banging and bellowing from inside the cage as the van takes off.

Eleven

The hospital is thick with shadows. A crush of colours and shapes melting in and out of each other, flow down fluorescent whitewashed halls. Outside the maternity ward, a shadow sits mid-air, feet up, as if lolling back in an armchair, reading a newspaper, awaiting good news. Passing the accident and emergency unit, shadow voices echo spent prayers, moans, and cries, while shadow doctors and nurses move about with harried footsteps and urgent voices...the air is rent with a fog of black and red shadows...

This place is alive. It is charged with bitter hope and despair, fierce love and loss.

Suzie and Toby move through these living halls—breathe the shadows into their lungs, their bloodstreams, their hearts. They cannot see the shadows, which reverberate with the histories that have begun and ended here, yet both feel them reverberate in their chest cavities. They take an elevator to the first floor—walk down another hallway—past the shadow of a middle-aged man curled in a ball, crying with abandon.

Suzie is following Toby. She trails him down a broad hallway, then right past the nurses' desk, into a ward. Toby doesn't stop at the desk—just keeps walking. The duty nurse, a young woman with a white shirt rolled up to the elbows and blue slacks, eyes Toby first, then Suzie: two dusty scarecrows. Suzie returns her stare and the nurse averts her gaze.

They continue down the length of the ward, passing rooms to their left and right—each room holding two or four patients—until they come to the room at the end.

'Michelle?'

Toby stops. Sitting on a suitcase outside the room is Michelle. She is wearing a Maccas uniform, just like Suzie, only hers is in pristine condition.

'Michelle?' Toby repeats. 'What're you doin' here?'

She wipes around her eyes.

'How's Danny?' Toby asks.

'Same as always.'

Toby says 'See ya' and pushes past, into the room.

Suzie lingers, sneering. She recognizes Michelle as the woman with the sunburnt breasts.

'Since when did you work f' Maccas?'

'I started this mornin'.'

'That prick! He sacked me so he could hire you.'

'You can keep it. I quit this mornin', too.'

'Good.'

Michelle takes her first decent look at Suzie.

'So, you're Toby's girlfriend?'

'Nah. He's my boyfriend.'

'As long as you know the difference. Cos they don't.'

Michelle lifts the suitcase with two hands, leans against its weight.

'Where're you going?'

'Away from here. I'm gunna go into the city an' see what happens. I just came here to say goodbye...I wanna be a hairdresser.'

'Fair enough.'

'Oh, yeah,' Michelle drops her voice. 'An' tell Toby I didn't tell them about him pinching Brendan's car, orright?'

'The cops?'

'Yeah. But I shoulda.'

Michelle says 'Bye' and starts walking away. Suzie calls 'Thanks' after her.

Twelve

'The bike's wrecked. I been tryin' to fix it, but.'

Suzie waits at the door, listening to Toby's hushed voice in the dim room.

'You could prob'ly fix it just like that,' Toby snaps his fingers.

Danny's room is the only one in the ward with the light off, the blinds shuttered against the sun—all Suzie sees are shadows and shapes.

'I'm just no good with engines. I never figured them out. I've fixed the front wheel, and welded a gusset to the frame. When you're up an' about—you know—you'll be able t'sort out the engine, get it kickin' over again.'

As Suzie's pupils dilate, the room materialises—a spartan affair with just a mattress in the middle of a lino floor. Two figures, one wearing filthy overalls, the other pyjama bottoms, are sitting on the mattress, facing away from her. Suzie goes round to the far side of the mattress, kneels on the floor before Danny.

'Danny? Danny? This is Suzie, Danny,' Toby says, then repeats *Suzie*.

He talks quietly, as though speaking to a sickly child.

'Hi!' Suzie says with forced enthusiasm.

Danny's head is lowered, his skin jaundiced and tight over his rib cage, his suede hair grown out; his tattoo of a flaming heart shrivelled on a matchstick arm. A pink scar protrudes between the notches of his collarbones, showing where the paramedics performed an emergency tracheotomy to keep him breathing. A plastic tube leads from his nostrils up to the drip.

So this is Danny, Suzie thinks. He smells like sour milk.

Toby touches Suzie's arm.

'What?'

'Say something.'

Danny is continually moving—like a slow motion replay, like a deep-sea diver, like a man on the moon. His right hand rises from his thigh as though levitating of its own accord, moves slowly, back and forth. A thread of saliva dangles from the corner of his shapeless mouth.

'Orright,' Suzie says.

She pulls a piece of motorbike debris from her pocket, places it in Danny's hands, once so sure of themselves, now blind to feeling. The chrome mirror clatters to the lino.

'Suzie,' Toby hisses.

'I wanna ask. You said I could.'

She retrieves the mirror, puts the chrome stem in Danny's open palm—says 'Look!' when the hand clenches the mirror in a fist.

'He's holding it. See?'

Just then Danny's fist relaxes and, once again, the mirror hits the floor.

Suzie gazes into Danny's eyes—two black holes with pupils blown wide open like fish-eye lenses—sees a brilliant yellow canvas, the reflection of the window blind backlit by the sun. A golden glow bleeds into the room.

Thirteen

A brilliant yellow canvas. That's what Danny sees, hears, feels, thinks, breathes and is. He is a canvas held up against the sun.

I see Danny riding his motorcycle—riding fast—screaming through the late afternoon—not thinking about anything—just riding—carving up the suburban streets around Another. Riding.

It is afternoon. Still and dry. The sun is flat against Danny's back.

A corner. Danny brakes, changes down, drops the bike into the corner—holding it off the hot bitumen with the counter-weight of his own body—takes the racing line.

The bike rights itself, accelerates out of that left, snaps into a sharp right, snarls down another gear.

Danny muscles the bike around the right-hander.

That corner wasn't as smooth as the left, but felt better, rougher—throwing the bike around—keeping the body in tune, like a spinnaker perfectly set to catch a stiff breeze.

Coming out of the corner the bike rights itself and jags ahead.

Danny hangs tight. Now the late afternoon sun hits him flush in the face—blinding him—and the world is brilliant yellow—hot air blasts against Danny's face.

His world is a short straight with a second tight right-hander at the end. Danny slits his eyes, but it makes no difference—all he can see is brilliant yellow. The bike's begging for speed—so Danny gives it throttle.

Danny's raced around this part of the estate dozens of times before—he has taken these corners in the dark, in the rain, even stoned and drunk—he loves the feel and sound of the bike—loves speed—riding hard until he can't feel himself—until it's as though he's flying. Like now—screaming blind into the sun. Danny starts coming down the gears. Knowing the right-hander's looming he steers with one hand—shields his eyes just long enough to sight the corner, chart his racing line. He starts to lean into the corner—lets the bike lean down low—shifts his weight to keep from coming off.

Then something goes wrong.

Beneath him, the wheels are slipping—going their own way, refusing to follow the racing line. Danny is in the apex of the corner—and he's losing it. The wheels are losing grip—sliding—and all he can do is hold on, lean harder.

Gravel. Danny hears it beneath the tyres—like ball-bearings on the road—as he starts to slide.

Fuck, he thinks. One of those builders must've spilt gravel on the road.

And he leans harder.

But then the tyres hit bitumen—bite—and the bike snaps upright—bucks—and he is half-flying, half-falling through the air—and all he can see is the brilliant yellow canvas of the sun.

It takes a considerable time to fall. A long fucking time. There is an eternity between being thrown from the bike and landing.

Danny is in suspended animation.

He is caught against the golden sky.

But he isn't scared.

Danny feels the sun and hot air against his face—and, as he tumbles, his eyes are wide open as though attempting to swallow the sun whole—and he thinks to himself, I lost it.

Breathe

One

The static inside Mum's head keeps her awake, keeps her brain turning over; keeps me awake, keeps me turning in my womb.

...Can't keep still...just can't...too tired—too tired to stop—too tired to sit, to sleep...too tired...knackered, actually...absolutely, positively can't sit still...fatigue is all over me, like ants on my face, in my head... I scratch at them, rattle round the kitchen, bathroom, bedroom, go out to the backyard—but nuthin' helps...poke around Toby's van...I'm lookin' for somethin'—what? what the fuck is it?...forget it...Jeez, it's hot...try the garage...up swings the garage door...Cooler...it's cooler in here...look at that, just look, all pulled apart and layin' there on the floor...fan-fucken-tastic...Toby tries to fix the bike an' he wrecks it, then he kicks the bejeezus outta the telly...nuthin' works—everything's broken...go back inside...try to forget, try to settle, get some sleep...Gran's dead—shit—Gran's dead an' lying on her bed all night like that...I should shut up that room, lock the lock so nuthin' gets in or outta there—nuthin'—or burn the bed, yeah, burn the thing...cos I'm not gunna sleep on it—no way...No way... Aw, Jeez—this joint stinks...stinks of fags and death and dust...this joint's a pressure cooker—slowly baking me from the inside out...what a shit-hole...I hate it...An' I hate Toby, too—hate him for making me worry about him...He never could take care of himself—goin' an' catching fire like that, an' the way he looked at me in the hospital with his back all raw... God, I wanted to throw up, find another match to light...An' now, Toby, you're back in trouble with the cops—animals, that's all they are...give 'em a gun and a badge and they grow an inch or two, don't they? Start throwing kids around in the back of their divi-vans...I know how it works...If that bastard gets his hands on you you'll know all about it, Toby...It's always a one-way street with cops—they never help you, but they can hurt you... An' they want me to hand over my son on a platter—bastards...Jeez, I'm buggered...need a tea...where's the kettle?—what a friggin' mess this is, Toby...Toby? where are you? look at the mess here—soggy crusts in the sink...shit...bugger the tea, I wanna sleep, if I could just get some sleep... Instead here I am, wearin' tracks in the carpet...

So she spends the remainder of the morning rearranging furniture in the lounge room, switching the couch and the TV around, sweeping the threadbare carpet.

Two

The day's heat—an intensity of light and humidity—has peaked. Suzie's sweltering in the leather jacket, but won't take it off; Toby's looking for a cold tap to shove his head under. They are standing at the intersection outside the hospital, staring at the Shoppingtown tower on the other side of the road, waiting for the lights to change.

'How long's he been like that?'

'A while,' Toby says.

Suzie's voice is soft, 'Is it a coma or something?'

'Or somethin'.'

Sick of standing still in the heat, they cross against the lights, thread their way through the Shoppingtown car park.

'So—has he got brain damage?'

'Guess so.'

'Oh.'

'Y'know, you may as well keep the mirror,' Toby says.

'Yeah?'

'Yeah. Cos it's no use to the bike anymore, anyway.'

Walking in step, Suzie and Toby cross the car park in silence, are swallowed up by Shoppingtown.

Three

Shoppingtown's air tingles—it's crisp, cold, like a giant frozen food section. The checkout chicks at Safeway wear T-shirts under their shirts to ward off the chill. Suzie and Toby meander about, mingle with the early afternoon crowd.

An old man is sitting on a bench sipping a jumbo cup of Coca-Cola. A middle-aged woman is sweeping the promenade. A toddler is throwing a tantrum outside the food court because his mother won't buy him an ice-cream. And there's a queue of three waiting to withdraw cash from the automatic teller machine.

Suzie and Toby check out the CD shop, poke through the rack of designer T-shirts on sale for fifty dollars in the surf shop, play free computer games in an electronics shop, ride up the down the escalators.

Suzie asks an old man for a smoke.

The man stops, cups a hand to his ear: 'What?'

'Smoke!' Suzie yells.

She makes a V with her fingers, presses them to her lips: 'Smoke! Do you have one?'

Shaking his head fervently, the man shuffles away.

'Oh, fuck,' Toby groans.

A security guard—a young man with brutally short hair, a square jaw and the build of a weightlifter—is making a beeline for them.

'Where's his moustache? I thought they all had moustaches,' Suzie says.

Toby starts laughing, sinks to the promenade and leans back against a jeweler's shop front. Jaw clenched, biceps bulging through his short shirtsleeves, the guard comes up, crosses his arms. Standing over Toby, he commands, 'Get up.'

'Why?' Suzie demands right back.

The guard ignores Suzie.

'Come on. Get up,' he tells Toby.

'What's the matter?' Suzie interjects. 'We haven't done anything wrong.'

Annoyed, the guard turns to Suzie: 'He can't sit here. That's the rules.'

'Who says?'

'Management says.'

Toby snorts derisively.

'Shut the fuck up,' the guard says.

'Why're you picking on us?' Suzie asks.

The guard stands there, arms folded, trying to come up with an adequate response; then gives up. Collaring Toby, he drags him across the ground, pulling him to his feet by his hair.

'Fuck! My hair! You've got my hair! Fuck!'

'Now get out,' the guard orders.

Suzie shoves the guard in the chest, 'You pulled him by the hair. That's fucken-well assault.'

'I didn't hurt him,' the guard protests.

Suzie gives the guard another shove: 'Bullshit! You can't throw us out. We're shopping.'

Grabbing Toby by the hand, Suzie marches towards the K-Mart at the far end of the promenade.

Keeping an indiscreet distance, the guard shadows Suzie and Toby as they weave through the men's wear, women's wear, and shoe sections. Suzie swerves back out into the promenade, dragging Toby in her wake—through a jean shop, then a bookstore. The guard loiters at the entrance of each shop they enter.

Hustling past, Suzie tells the guard to piss off. She and Toby take the up-escalator. On the down-escalator, gliding towards them, is an Aborigine. This man, a Koori, is well into his middle age, yet still lithe, with only the trace of a belly under his faded Mabo T-shirt. He is a striking sight—the only black man in the shopping centre. The Koori's eyes glint, catching Toby's grey eyes as he passes by, gliding down towards the bookstore. Standing at the bottom of the escalators, the security guard is confounded when he notices the Koori. He hesitates, slaps his thigh as he tries to make a security decision. The Koori steps off the escalator, walks into the bookstore. Glancing up at Toby and Suzie who have now stepped off the escalator, the guard makes his decision about which situation is more pressing—two renegade teenagers or an Aboriginal in a bookstore. He lingers, then steps into the bookstore.

Four

Mum feels herself melt into the water. The bath is scalding hot, with just a dash of the cold tap. Reaching with a lazy arm, she finds her mug of tea, sips: compared to the bath water, the brew tastes cold.

...Is this what it's like, being dead?—left alone, in peace at last, with nobody knocking at the door, or is it nothin'—just darkness...Who cares? I'm here now—alive—sweating good clean sweat...that's better than nothin'...look at my fingers, all shrivelled up by the water—a prune—stay put much longer an' I'll look like a sultana...all the life left in me will dissolve into the water, go down the spout...Jeez, I'm worn down—worn paper-thin...I need to sleep. Why can't I sleep?...Maybe I should dye my hair instead—run some henna through to hide the grey streaks, so it shines burgundy-brown in the sun...that'd be nice...tired—Jeez, I'm just bone-dead-tired...

With that thought, Mum dozes off. And, as she slips to sleep, her mug submerges, her lukewarm tea colouring the hot clean water...

Five

Another day is dying.

The sun rises, the sun peaks, the sun subsides—indifferent to the lives played out beneath its gaze. I see this day dying—the feeding of the heat and dust—and find myself in love with this day for no good reason.

Perhaps it is because of the horizon.

Traffic must have been heavy in the city today—cars stewing at traffic lights, crawling along the freeway, the fumes knitting, cooking all afternoon in the sun, dividing and blending and mutating until the sun sank, refracting the cocktail of diesel particles, carbon dioxide, and benzene, setting the sky aflame.

The sky is on fire—a plume of ochre and rose and maroon—and the high, corrugated clouds are rendered golden by the sinking sun. This evening there are colours within colours—afire—twisting and melting into each other. Subtle colours and gentle light stretch long warm shadows across Another, etch out the high-voltage power lines starkly, against the horizon. The navigational lights of 747s and 737s blink brightly, heat waves shimmering across the sky from the stream of their turbine engines.

It is another day. And, although I love this day, it does not matter; it still dies. As the sun sets, I see its final images: black and purple shadows unwinding from the earth.

Six

The water is cold when Mum wakes. She is still grasping the submerged mug of tea with a dead-woman's grip. She pulls the plug. Stands up. Drips dry. Steps out of the bath and rummages through the hallway cupboard.

Where's my good towel? Shit—Suzie's got it.

Mum grabs a towel, once white, now thin and grey, and goes back to the bathroom; dries herself properly, rubs the towel over the wet floor with her foot, steps up to the mirror.

That day in the supermarket, when Danny and Toby were kids, the sight of Gary gave Jacki an electric shock, sent her reeling. She caught just a flicker of him standing at the end of the aisle in his work boots, hands on hips—but a flicker was enough. Jacki didn't hang around to see what happened next. She grabbed the kids and bolted—crazy with fear, wild with anger—finding her way to the car park through the supermarket's storage room.

She unlocked the driver's door, flung Toby between the bucket seats, into the back. Danny started to say something, but Jacki screamed 'Get in!'—pushed the boy over the driver's console, sent the car squealing out of the car park.

'Shouldn't we have our seatbelts on?' Danny asked.

Scanning the rearview mirror, Jacki steadied her voice, 'It's all right today. You don't have to wear your seatbelts today.'

But all the while Jacki was cursing herself: I should've killed him in his sleep. I should've taken that carving knife, the good one, and gutted the bastard. Too late, now. Now he's found us, fuck him.

Jacki was wild. She'd left Gary after Pa died—staying in a caravan park until she talked Gran into selling her house and buying a cheap subdivision in Another, a place so far away from the peninsula and Gary it seemed like the dark side of the moon. She'd cut her hair short, kept a silent phone number, refused to tell people her last name, lost contact with her few friends. It had been years since she'd seen him—since that day she packed the car and took off with the week's shopping money in her jeans.

But now Gary'd found her.

Jacki went on alert. Every creak and groan in the house, every passing car, was Gary. One night she was sure she heard footsteps out on the gravel drive, so she got up, clasping a knife to her side, and crept around the house, checking every room, hovering over Danny and Toby in their beds. Turning on the outside light, she searched the driveway. Circled the house. Nothing. If it had been him he could be anywhere now. He could have jumped the fence and been swallowed up by the darkness. Jacki couldn't sleep. She kept the outside light on, went back inside, made herself a cup of tea, waited.

Gran came out and sat down at the table, glared at her daughter: 'You woke me up.'

'I saw him today,' Jacki said.

'Gawd. Is that all you woke me up for?'

'Go back to bed.'

Jacki waited until Gran shuffled off, then called the police—told the weary voice at the other end of the line what had happened.

'It was probably nothing,' the voice yawned.

'How d'you know? I'm the one that heard it.'

'Uh-huh.'

'What's that mean?'

'Nothing—look, lock all your doors and go back to bed, we'll check the area for prowlers.'

'But I toldja who did it. Aren't y'gunna arrest him?'

'What for? Interrupting your beauty sleep?'

'What for?! For beating me up.'

'When? Tonight?'

'No. When I was with him.'

'And when was that exactly?'

'A while ago...A few years back.'

'Uh-huh...Look, just do as I said, orright? Lock the doors, go to sleep and let us keep an eye on things.' *Click*.

Mum stares at the bathroom mirror, but isn't looking at her reflection—she is staring at the shadow behind her. *Him*.

Slamming the bathroom door shut behind her, Mum runs out the front door, wrapped in a soggy, grey-white towel.

Jacki patrolled the house. Armed with her knife, she did circuits of the house, conducted head counts every hour—kept the outside light blazing. As the nights wore on, though, her conviction faded—she found it harder to stay awake.

On the last night, Jacki stood at the bottom of the drive and called out to Gary: 'Come an' get me you useless gutless bastard.'

And...nothing. He wasn't there.

Jacki felt the tension leach from her in a sigh. The knife felt ridiculous in her hand—embarrassing—and Jacki had an overwhelming urge to drop to the ground and sleep, make up for all the restless nights. Perhaps it hadn't been Gary at the supermarket, after all.

Stifling a yawn, she trudged slowly up the flood-lit driveway, listening to the gravel crunch beneath her feet. As she neared the front steps, another hurried noise started coming out of the darkness from behind her. An alarming noise. Heavy footsteps running up the drive.

She spun around.

It was Gary. He was carrying a jerry can and a shotgun. He was wearing the work boots and jeans he had worn in the supermarket as he came running towards her, pounding up the drive.

The gravel is warm and sharp against the soles of Mum's bare feet.

It's dusk. Although the colours of the sky are still incandescent, they are beginning to lose their lustre as the sun slips away.

Something is moving inside the house. Mum can see the shadow through the lounge room window.

Gary flattened Jacki, jabbing the butt of the rifle into her face, breaking her nose.

The knife—she dropped it and he scooped it up. Blood was all over her hands, her T-shirt, her face, as he dragged her inside.

'Get my boys,' he ordered.

'Useless gutless bastard,' Jacki whispered.

He dragged Jacki kicking and screaming into Gran's bedroom, booted the old woman awake and told her to bring the boys out to the kitchen.

'Bring 'em straight out or she's dead,' Gary said—speaking in a detached, superior tone, as if to say Jacki had failed to adequately perform one of her duties and was now suffering the consequences.

Gary sat himself on a chair in the middle of the kitchen with Jacki at his feet, a knife held to her throat.

In came Gran, carrying a drowsy Toby on her hip. Danny followed behind.

'Danny,' Gary said affectionately. 'Good to see you boy-o. Bring me that can.'

'Don't hurt them,' Jacki pleaded.

'Show me Toby.'

Gran sat Toby on the lino.

'He looks like his old man, doesn't he?' Gary declared happily, then called out to Danny. 'You got that can, Danny boy?'

'Yep!' Danny called back from the lounge.

'Good. Now take the lid off and start pouring it on the carpet in the lounge and the hallway, orright?'

'Pour it? But it smells funny.'

'Do as y'told.'

'This is my house,' Gran muttered.

'Dry up,' Gary ordered.

Pushing Jacki away with a kick between the shoulder blades, Gary picked up Toby, sat him on his lap.

'Toby!' he said proudly. 'You're gettin' big, Toby boy.'

He tousled Toby's hair with the same hand that held the knife.

'I'm nearly finished,' Danny called from the lounge.

'Good. Bring what's left in here, boy-o.'

Danny hauled the jerry can in, plonked it on the lino.

'Pour it out on the floor.'

'Don't,' Jacki pleaded.

'Do it.'

Danny looked at his mother, looked at his father—hesitated—then emptied the jerry can on the lino floor. Petrol fumes stung Jacki's nostrils.

The house is on fire again. Shadow flames lick the walls of the house, ripple across the roof—red and orange and black and grey—billow into the night. Mum can smell the fire, hear shadow voices calling 'Toby! Tow-bee!'—can see a boy shadow smouldering in the sandbox—and, despite herself, long dead images of that night re-ignite: come alive again, burn again.

...Jacki lunging at Gary...Gary dropping the knife and Jacki grabbing it...Gary punching Jacki...Jacki stabbing Gary in the chest, the throat, the face...And blood...blood all over the floor, mingling with the petrol...and Gary's expression, calm determination, as she stabbed him...*Click!*—then the sound of his lighter striking...and fire...

Mum has tried to forget the night her world caught fire.

Treading carefully through the backyard, Mum stops at the sandbox, crouches over, reaches out to touch the boy shadow, but her fingers pass through the glass skin.

Standing, Mum walks into the van, sits on Toby's dishevelled bed, rubs her shins as if warding off a chill, lies on the grubby sheets. She wants desperately to sleep.

Seven

Toby is staring out the window at the luminous sky. As it subsides the sky is on fire. As the bus takes the looping exit from the freeway into Another, he cannot take his eyes from the sunset. Suzie pulls the cord and the bus winds down the gears until it comes to a stop across from McDonald's. Suzie and Toby disembark, stand in the dusk as the bus lurches back into traffic with its exhaust belching smoke, tyres kicking up a cloud of dust. By the time the bus is in second gear Toby is already halfway across the road—standing on the double lines as cars dodge around him, slashing his legs with the glare of their headlights. The traffic feeding into Another from the freeway eases, lets Suzie join Toby on the double lines. She stands close to him, balancing on the balls of her feet. He feels her beside him and, without taking his eyes from the oncoming traffic, finds her hand. They hold onto each other just like good children do when crossing the road.

Three more cars career past—tug at Suzie and Toby's clothes. Another bus bears down—its wheels slipping over the double lines as it struggles to contain its bulk to one side of the road.

There is a narrow gap between the third car and the oncoming bus. Suzie squeezes Toby's hand, and, with perfect timing, they run for the safety of the roadside as the bus blasts by—*BAAAOOOMPH!*—cuffing their backs with a wave of hot air.

Eight

Toby asks Suzie what she is thinking.

'I'm thinking I'm gunna die if I don't have a smoke.'

They're sitting on the bonnet of a Falcon station-wagon, watching the people troop in and out of McDonald's. All the seats are taken and more people than usual are lining up inside because the Drive-Thru's still out of order.

'D'you reckon I should ask for my job back?' Suzie asks.

'No way. He should ask you back.'

'Yeah. So what're we gunna do?'

'We'll think of something.'

'It'd be good if we could buy a plane ticket to New York. My Mum'd meet us there f'sure.'

'New York?'

'Yeah—we could do lots of stuff there.'

'Has your Mum been to New York?'

Suzie nods: 'Sure has.'

The fire in the sky has flickered out. Shadows congregate around the electric islands of the servo and McDonald's, kiss the dirty faces of Toby and Suzie—causing them to lick their lips, scratch their cheeks with grimy fingers.

'I'm starvin,' Suzie says.

'Me too,' Toby replies.

A boy wearing baggy shorts and shirt, with a Chicago Bulls cap on backwards, walks past, chewing on a cheeseburger. The unmistakable sugary smell makes Toby swallow. He calls after the boy, trying to sound friendly, but the boy keeps walking.

'Hey!'

Toby jumps off the Falcon and the boy bolts, colliding head-on with a parked Corona in a panic, spilling his soft drink over its windscreen.

'Hey!'

Toby jogs after the boy, who is now frantically limping away, before returning to the Falcon empty-handed.

'Fuck! Why couldn't he've drop his cheeseburger?' he says.

'Why couldn't he've dropped a smoke,' Suzie replies.

Nine

Beepbeep! Beepbeep! **THE POLICE SAY U STOLE A CAR. DID TOBY PUT U UP 2 THIS?**

'What d'you think Danny thinks about?' Suzie asks.

A reflection of the servo's neon sign burns in Toby's eye.

'What d'you mean?'

'He's alive. He's sitting there with his eyes open. So—y'know—he must think about stuff.'

They've been staking out the servo—watching from the edge of the paddock, out of the light—for more than an hour.

'What's he thinking about?'

Toby is astounded. He has never considered the possibility that Danny is in anything other than suspended animation.

'Yeah.'

'Jeez—I dunno. Prob'ly nuthin.'

'Why?'

'Well—he landed on his fucken head, didn't he? He's probably like a punch drunk boxer. Can't think straight.'

'Is that what you think?'

Toby rubs his nose, 'I dunno. Maybe.'

'So why do you go see him then?'

'Jeez!' Toby exclaims. 'He's still Danny, isn't he? He's still my brother.'

They wait in silence for McDonald's to close, for the cars pulling into the servo to thin out.

Finally, the servo is deserted, the cashier alone.

'You right to do this?'

Toby doesn't reply.

'I can come and help.'

'Nup.'

'Y'sure?'

Toby stands, 'Look. I can do it, orright? Where're the pantyhose at?'

'At the back.'

'Okay,' he tries to sound calm. 'Wait here. Don't budge.'

He starts marching towards the servo.

'Toby?' Suzie hisses.

He turns around: 'Yeah?'

'Can you get me some smokes, too?'

'Fuck!'

He starts jogging towards the servo before she can ask for anything else.

Ten

Humm-shh. As the automatic door shushes closed behind him Toby ducks behind an aisle, scuttles across to the back corner of the store—a blind spot directly beneath the video surveillance camera. Crouched amongst the shelves of tampons, med-pads and pantyhose, Toby's hummingbird heart is thumping in his ears.

...Breathe...Breathe deep now...that's better...where are they? fuck—they're not here—where are they?...there: Sheer Silk Pantyhose...which colour, but?...who gives a shit—take one...good...open it...will it fit? doesn't look big enough...don't put it on yet, but...No...hang on—breathe—keep out of sight...who's at the counter? Is it bug eyes?...Yeah—that prick...the arse-hole who goes, *It's not a fucken library*...Nah. It's not a library, it's a bank...Whose bank? My fucken bank...

Crouched over, back to the surveillance camera, Toby prowls the aisles, searching for a weapon. Behind the counter, the preying mantis squints at the distant blur, tries to figure out whether it's a man or a woman in the car-care section.

...Charged and ready to go...Charged an' ready to go...Charged an' fucken well ready to go...Here I go...

Toby finds a weapon, braces, tells himself to breathe deeply once more, then advances on the counter.

Eleven

At 11:12.45 on the video surveillance camera's twelve-hour clock, an armed robber enters its grainy, black-and-white field of vision. The offender is approximately 172 centimetres tall, Caucasian, fair-haired, with a slight build, aged between 18 and 25, wearing overalls, disguised with a pair of women's pantyhose over his head and armed with an anti-car theft device commonly known as a club-lock.

'Money! Give me money!' the offender demands—running up and striking the counter with the club-lock.

'Hang on,' the cashier says, but is cut short.

'Money now! Now! This is my fucken bank!'

Police later describe the offender as extremely agitated and nervous, possibly a drug addict. Confused, the cashier—a forty-two-year-old father of three—nods, opens the register, pulls out some fives, a ten, a twenty.

'Is that all?!'

The cashier nods again.

'Count it.'

The cashier complies: 'Five. Ten. Twenty. Twenty-five. Forty-five.'

Now the offender is screaming: 'No! I need a hundred! A hundred bucks! More—gimme more!'

The cashier says, 'It's here, I'll get it,' and, bending over, reaches under the counter.

That's when—in an act police call savage, cowardly and unprovoked—the offender strikes the cashier across the back of the head with the club-lock.

The force of the blow fractures the cashier's skull. Unconscious, he collapses beneath the camera's view. The offender vaults the counter, stands over the cashier.

The surveillance tape records what next transpires. The offender raises his arm and brings the club-lock down hard and fast, repeatedly; an intensity of violence blurring itself across the tape. After what seems like an eternity, the offender breaks away, looks around, takes forty-five dollars from the till and decamps from the scene of the crime on foot. The camera reads 11:15.41 when the offender exits the servo.

The aggravated-armed robbery has taken less than three minutes.

Twelve

Breathebreathebreathebreathebreathe...

Frantic, Toby sprints for the perimeter of the servo and the safety of darkness—listening to the blood pound through his head.

The pantyhose are choking him, blinding him, but he cannot stop. So intent on escape is Toby he forgets the fence; runs full-pelt into the barbed wire.

'Fuck!'

The wire stops him dead, bites deep into his chest and right thigh.

'Stand still!' Suzie orders.

She tries to calm Toby, who is weeping for breath, as she untangles, then drags, him over the fence.

Bleeding and winded, he falls onto the hard paddock floor.

'You orright?'

Toby shakes his head, fights for air. Suzie leans over, pulls the pantyhose from his head.

'What happened? Didja get money?'

He nods.

'Let's go, then.'

Suzie grabs Toby's arm, drags him into the long grass and the shadows.

'Hurry,' she says.

Toby is wheezing to keep up with Suzie. She is leading him by the hand as they stumble together through the darkness like good children crossing the road.

Suzie leading, Toby following, they plough through grass and thistle—brush past shadows, keep on the fringes of Another, run beside Hanlon's electric fence—beneath the high-voltage power lines and the stars.

They run until they reach the edge of their world.

Dreams

One

Suzie can no longer ignore me. She sees me now—she dreams me—and I dream her.

Mother. If I could speak, that would be my first word. What would her first word to me be?

I see myself as Suzie sees me—a fist of scar tissue growing in her womb. That image makes me curl into a ball, wish to close my mind's eye, cease to exist. In her dream, Suzie lies alone in the long dry grass, directly beneath a midday sun.

She is naked.

Her belly is swollen.

And she is holding her razor.

Suzie is wondering how deep she will have to cut to wake herself.

Two

It's early when Mum wakes, disorientated, in Toby's bunk. Pale sunlight spills through the van's door. It is morning.

She covers herself with the grey-white towel, sits on the step of the van with her knees together. It is early, and, already, the day smells scorched.

I thought I buried you.

That thought is on a relay loop, replaying in Mum's head as she dresses quickly in her bedroom—pulling on shorts, runners, a T-shirt, arming herself with a knife.

With the weapon in her hand, Mum no longer feels naked. She searches inside—under beds, through cupboards and wardrobes, up in the ceiling—circles outside the house. Nothing.

I thought I buried you. Christ, I should've gutted you when I had the chance, you useless gutless bastard.

She ends up in the kitchen: standing where Gary lay that night, bleeding from his wounds, as Jacki stabbed at him. This is the very spot where her world caught fire.

It all started here. I thought it ended here, but it didn't. All it did was fuck my boys—send them the wrong way down a one-way street. I should've fucken killed you in your sleep, Gary. It might've stopped just with me, then. It might have. It's too late, now, but—too late—the damage's done an' it's still paying out on us. Another day, another kick in the head.

Mum picks up a box of matches sitting on the windowsill, slides it open, picks out a match, strikes it, holds it between her thumb and forefinger; lets the fire burn right down to her fingertips.

Three

If the underbelly of the 747 is the sky, the sky is falling.

Pinned flat to the earth, Suzie waits until the jet lumbers over and lets the blue sky back in, then jumps to her feet. The monster hangs so low its wheels cannot possibly clear the cyclone wire fence.

Safely over the perimeter fence, air-brakes on, wings tremoring, the 747 touches down—a chalk squawk and puffs of smoke rises from its wheels as they kiss the tarmac.

Fingering the wire fence, Suzie yawns with relief—the plane is down and her belly is not the size of a watermelon. Not yet. She feels her stomach—a barely discernible swelling pressing against the palm of her hand—and sees an image: Suzie and Toby fucking beneath an open sky.

'Where are we?' Toby asks.

He's finally awake. Suzie has been watching him sleep for the past half-hour—rolling in the grass, grunting and twitching.

'The airport,' Suzie replies.

'We ran that far?'

'Yep.'

He sits upright.

'You orright?' she asks.

He simply slags in the dirt, rubs his face.

'Lovely,' Suzie says.

'You don't look so shit-hot, neither.'

'Look at this.'

Toby stands beside Suzie. Together, they watch a 747 lumber up the runway towards them, slowly drawing momentum and speed until, with a hundred metres to go, its nose lifts as though pulled into the sky by an invisible hand. With the nose airborne, the tail quickly follows, sending the metal monolith into a sharp climb away from the earth, into the clear sky above Another.

'Shit, eh?'

'Yeah,' Toby says and sits down.

'You sure you're orright?'

'Sure I'm sure...I'm just hungry.'

Suzie gives him a dubious look, changes the subject: 'I had a dream last night.'

'Oh? I thought you never dreamed.'

'Well, I did.'

'And what'd y'dream about?'

'Well, what'd you dream about? You first.'

Toby stares at his feet, 'I didn't dream.'

'Bullshit.'

'I didn't.'

'Oh, yeah. So I s'pose you tossed around cos you felt like it.'

'...Yeah.'

'Piss off.'

'Suzie.'

She turns away.

'Go on, Suzie. Tell me what you dreamed about.'

'I was gunna tell you,' she says. 'I was. But now y'gunna have to wait.'

'Till when?'

'Till I make up my mind.'

Four

Toby and Suzie brush the dirt from their clothes, pry bindi-eyes from their hair, and start walking. They follow the airport's fence line until they hit a road. Follow that road past bitumen paddocks crammed with parked cars, until they are outside the main entrance of the airport's international terminal.

Here it's rush hour—elbow-to-elbow stand businesspeople and holiday-makers queuing for departure, as well as families welcoming red-eyed arrivals. Dazed by the crush, Suzie and Toby are swept into the terminal.

Just inside the main entrance is a rectangular foyer with a sliding door in the middle of the longest wall. Two Plexiglas corridors feed from that sliding door to opposite ends of the foyer. Above the sliding door is an international ARRIVALS board.

This foyer is packed with people of every race and creed. Some sit on the floor, others stand chattering in groups, still others press themselves against the Plexiglas, trying to catch the first glimpse of their passenger, or crane their necks to study the ARRIVALS board in the hope that the flight they are awaiting will click over and read LANDED.

As Toby and Suzie manoeuvre through the crowd, the sliding door opens. A teenager no older than Suzie, just cleared by Customs, exits, inexpertly steering his luggage trolley. He is a young man dressed in a black single-breasted suit, with a white shirt buttoned to the throat and a skull cap perched on the back of his head. His pale, flawless face is framed with braided black pigtails. Waiting for this young man, waving at him enthusiastically, is a crowd of similarly clad men, except they are older and have long beards that are black or grey or white. One man, bowed and frail, but sporting the whitest beard, stands at the front of the welcoming party recording the happy moment on his video camera—the flashing red RECORD light catches Suzie's eye as she passes.

Five

'I thought you were hungry,' Suzie says to Toby.

They've taken the escalator up to the galleria, wandered round the shops—buffeted by throngs of people with places to go—and strayed into a duty-free shop long enough for Suzie to try on six pairs of Bolle sunglasses and tell a miffed sales assistant 'Get fucked.'

Now they are standing in the middle of the galleria as trolleys loaded with luggage, backpackers, uniformed airline crew, and business people dodge them on either side.

'We need the money.'

'What for?'

'Your board. Remember?'

'We don't even have half of it, but. I'm still rooted.'

People brush past, reminding Suzie of the night before—how she and Toby stood on the road outside McDonald's, holding hands, waiting for a break in the traffic. Poised on the balls of her feet, Suzie waits for a break in the throng, pushes through.

'Suzie,' Toby calls—struggling to catch up.

'Get me some cigarettes,' she orders and heads for the toilets.

Six

Suzie locks herself in a cubicle, kneels before the toilet bowl with her elbows resting on the seat, head in her hands.

She stays that way for a long while, as though in prayer, then throws up.

Kneeling there, Suzie massages her aching stomach, inspects the watery sick in the bowl, then slags, wipes her mouth.

Beepbeep! Beepbeep! **SUZIE, THE POLICE CAME LOOKING 4 TOBY & U. I TOLD THEM HE'S TAKEN U HOSTAGE. CALL ME. DAD.**

'Fuck!' Suzie yells.

She dumps the mobile in the toilet—flushes—watches her spew and the mobile spin and clatter round together before they are sucked down the S-bend by the vortex of water.

Knock, knock.

'Are you OK? Hello?' a woman's voice asks from outside the cubicle.

Suzie sees a pair of stockinged feet clad in black-patent leather pumps under the dunny door.

'Mum?' she says and throws open the door.

Attached to those patent-leather pumps is a forty-something woman with a black bob. The woman smiles at the weather-beaten teenager.

'Is everything all right? I'm afraid I'm not your mother.'

Suzie's face is about to shift from hopeful to an even more exposed expression when it contorts, twists out a violent: 'Get fucked!'

Slamming the cubicle shut, Suzie sits on the toilet until the woman, still speechless, scuttles out.

Seven

A long mirror stretches across the length of the wash basins. Suzie is standing at the centre basin, washing her hands.

She assesses herself in the mirror. Her hair is a bird's nest, her eyes bloodshot, her face bruised above her right eyebrow, the flesh around her right eye appears as though coloured-in with shaded crayon.

'You look like shit,' Suzie tells herself.

She splashes water around her throat, washes her face, pulls her hair back into a ponytail, takes off Danny's leather jacket, unbuttons the bloodstained McDonald's shirt and has her first decent look at the rose. It is black and tender, an arrangement of dried blood and tortured flesh.

Suzie soaks a paper towel. Dabs at the rose. Fingers the scar. Likes its ragged symmetry. She is picking at a scab when another woman enters the toilets, stands to attention at the neighbouring basin. This woman is younger than the one with the patent-leather pumps—a tall blonde in new jeans and a white bodysuit. She makes a half-hearted attempt to wash her hands, but is unable to take her eyes off Suzie's wound.

'D'you like it?' Suzie asks.

'Excuse me?' the woman feigns confusion.

Suzie smiles: 'It's my rose. I've been watering it.'

The woman leaves without drying her hands.

Eight

Toby is loitering outside the toilets, polishing off a Quarter Pounder, wiping his hands on Danny's overalls. He likes Danny's overalls, likes the way they fit him, make him feel; likes the way they remind him of Danny.

Last night seems unreal to Toby. All night, lying beside the cyclone-wire fence, Toby tried to come to terms with what he'd done.

All night he relived the robbery. Saw himself standing over the cashier, hitting him with the club-lock. It felt good, hitting him. It felt powerful. Each blow was a liberation: an expression. But an expression of what? The fire? Danny? *Something* is all Toby knows. He struck out and struck down a man, hit something made of flesh and bone—not memories—and no longer felt so helpless. He heard the sound of the metal striking the man's skull, felt the blow jar up his arm—and his head went light with a surge of adrenaline. So he did it again. He hit the cashier again and again, and, no matter how many times he hit the cashier, the feeling didn't change. Last night he hurt a man, possibly killed a man, and it felt good.

Suzie finally exits the toilets.

'You hungry?'

'I hate McDonald's,' she says—but takes his fries anyway, shovelling them into her mouth three and four at a time.

'I didn't know what y'wanted. We can go back an' get somethin'.'

'Later,' she says.

Toby swallows the last morsel of the burger, slurps on his Coke as Suzie finishes his fries.

'I'm still hungry,' he tells her.

Suzie nods: 'An' I'd kill for a smoke.'

'Here you go, then.'

He tosses Suzie a packet of Peter Jackson, which she snatches in mid-air, eagerly tugging at the plastic wrapper.

'Not in here.'

'What?'

'It's not allowed. The cops'd come if we smoked here.'

'Fuck.'

They wander the airport until they find the observation deck—a narrow verandah on top of the galleria with a view across the runway, towards Another.

It is warm out on the deck. The morning sun slaps Suzie and Toby in the face. They squint, shade their eyes with their hands. A conga-line of smokers slumps against the deck's rail, watching a 737 taxi for take-off.

Suzie pokes a cigarette into the corner of her mouth, pats herself down for a light.

'Fuck,' she says. 'Fuck.'

'What now?'

'You didn't buy matches didja?'

Toby turns his pockets inside out, finding no matches, but rediscovers the gold chain he stole from the house with the baby. He holds the chain up against the sky, its gold glitters in the sun.

'This is for you.'

The chain curls into the palm of Suzie's hand.

'D'you like it?'

'Yeah. It's real pretty.'

She clips the chain around her neck, pecks Toby on the corner of his mouth, which is greasy with food.

'Where'd you get it?'

'I found it.'

Nearby, a Lebanese taxi driver is smoking a cigarillo extravagantly, watching Suzie and Toby. She catches his eye, smiles.

'S'cuse me? Could I have a light?'

The driver shrugs, and in one fluid motion flips the lid off his Zippo, sparks it alight. Suzie leans close, lets the man touch her arm as she waits for her cigarette to draw. Toby holds back, notices the man touching Suzie, vaguely contemplates whether he should head-butt the prick as soon as he steps away from Suzie.

Nine

I feel the impact of the cigarette almost immediately—red blood turns blue—my images lose focus—my head goes dizzy from lack of oxygen. And I kick.

You and I are separate parts of the same body, Suzie. We are the same flesh and blood. We are forged by the same fire; synchronized by the same heart.

And I know now that you feel me inside you.

I kick again.

Ten

For the umpteenth time, Suzie massages her stomach with an open palm. She is certain she feels something—a twinge. Is that a good sign? Hand on her belly, she glances at Toby, but he hasn't noticed her grimace. It is becoming a reflex action, this rubbing and petting. It is getting harder to ignore.

Suzie sags against the rail, smokes her smoke.

Toby, having decided against head-butting the taxi driver, is beside her. Whenever Toby turns his face away from Suzie, she turns towards him—narrows her eyes at him as though trying to come to some conclusion. Her head swims with dark colours and smoke.

'Look,' Toby says.

He is pointing at the high voltage power lines marching along the horizon, towards Another. Suzie shields her eyes with the back of her hand.

Through the slits of her eyes, Suzie sees the column of black smoke rising. She sees the smoke and knows that somewhere, somewhere close, there is a fire.

Also in The Emerging Authors Series

An Accident in the Evening*, Phil Brown*
ISBN 187681909X, $22

Bacchanalia*, B.R. Dionysius*
ISBN 187681912X, $22

Café Boogie*, Jenni Nixon*
ISBN 1876819200, $23

Cry Ma Ma to the Moon*, Lesley Singh*
ISBN 1876819138, $22

Frankenstein's Bathtub*, Tricia Dearborn*
ISBN 1876819073, $19.75

I'll Howl Before You Bury Me*, Liam Guilar*
ISBN 1876819170, $23

Joyflight*, Cate Kennedy*
ISBN 187681926X, $23

minorphysics*, Paul Mitchell*
ISBN 1876819170, $23

Swelter*, Louise Waller & Kristin Hannaford*
ISBN 1876819146, $23

Terminal Velocity*, Molly Guy*
ISBN 1876819197, $23

For the latest from Interactive Press, Glass House Books and IP Digital, please visit IP on the Net at http://www.ipoz.biz/store/store.htm or contact us by phone at 61 7 3395 0269